*A strong arm wound about Latina's neck. She felt herself being dragged up through the swirling water to the blessed sunshine. Coughing and spluttering, she clung to Tully as he lifted her to the bank. He set her gently on the sun-baked rock and hefted himself beside her.*

*"A whirlpool," he exclaimed amid heavy gasps for air. "Sorry I had to grab you like that! It happened too fast for me to warn you."*

*Gradually she began to breathe more evenly. He placed his hand over hers and bent over her. "I almost—" his voice caught "—I almost lost you."*

*Through half-closed eyes, she watched his face come closer to hers. She felt his lips gently brush her forehead. "Latina, my Latina, you gave me a terrible fright."*

Dear Readers:

Thank you for your unflagging interest in First Love From Silhouette. Your many helpful letters have shown us that you have appreciated growing and stretching with us, and that you demand more from your reading than happy endings and conventional love stories. In the months to come we will make sure that our stories go on providing the variety you have come to expect from us. We think you will enjoy our unusual plot twists and unpredictable characters who will surprise and delight you without straying too far from the concerns that are very much part of all our daily lives.

We hope you will continue to share with us your ideas about how to keep our books your very First Loves. We depend on you to keep us on our toes!

Nancy Jackson
Senior Editor
FIRST LOVE FROM SILHOUETTE

# BLOSSOM INTO LOVE
## Norma Jean Lutz

*First Love from Silhouette*

Published by Silhouette Books New York

**America's Publisher of Contemporary Romance**

SILHOUETTE BOOKS
300 E. 42nd St., New York, N.Y. 10017

ISBN: 0-373-06167-6

First Silhouette Books printing December 1985
Second printing January 1986

America's Publisher of Contemporary Romance

Printed in the U.S.A.

RL 6.0, IL Age 11 and up

**NORMA JEAN LUTZ** lives with her husband and two teenagers near Tulsa, Oklahoma, where she has the best of two worlds. She can look out her back patio doors and see miles of rolling tree-covered hills, but she is also close to the city. In addition to writing and teaching writing to adults, Ms. Lutz raises her own cattle.

# Chapter One

Latina Harmen knew she was going to hate Missouri. "There's *nothing* in Missouri!" she had told her father when he announced they were to spend the summer there. And now she knew she had been one hundred and ten percent right.

The Harmen's family car lurched and swayed around each sharp hairpin curve deep in the green-black Ozark mountains. As the dense stands of trees flew by, Latina had been watching the curving roads and valleys directly beneath the road. But now she was unable to look out the window at all.

The usually sweet fragrance of her father's pipe was making her feel sick. She pressed her forehead against the cool window and squeezed her eyes shut. She

couldn't have motion sickness. Latina, the girl w
fearlessly rode the wildest rides at the ocean-front par
in Periwinkle Cove each and every summer? Impos
sible.

Her thirteen-year-old brother, Dirk had finally
stopped his nerve-shattering habit of snapping the little rubber bands on his braces and was now gazing out
his window at the panoramic view offering a few in-
telligent comments such as "Wow!" and "Gee whiz,
would you look at that!"

His very excitement over this desolate place was
more than enough to nauseate Latina even without the
constant, unending rocking of the car.

She clenched her teeth in a determined effort not to
be sick in the car like a little kid. As she did, a soft
uncontrollable moan escaped her lips.

Dirk turned to look at her. "Hey Mom! Latina's
making like Casper the Ghost!"

In a sort of haze, she heard her mother saying to her
father, "Oh Ross! She's car sick. How much farther?"

"We turn off the main highway about five miles up
ahead, but then it's seven more miles to Zell's Bush."

Latina's mother looked into the back seat, con-
cerned for her daughter. "Think you can hold on that
long, Latina?"

Latina nodded without unclenching her teeth. The
hamburger she'd had at lunch felt as if it was hanging
somewhere in the halfway spot in her esophagus.

Zell's Bush. Even the name of the town to which they were headed was revolting. Every new lurch of the car took her farther and farther from the beach at Periwinkle Cove. And from Kent Starner.

As far as she could see out across the valleys, there were hills of deep green pine, which looked almost black—black and ominous. It seemed like an eternity before they turned a tight little curve on the dusty back road and saw a huddle of buildings sitting just past a sign announcing: Zell's Bush. POP. 381.

Professor Ross Harmen parked and took long strides up the wooden steps to the high porch of a store whose faded sign read *Boles's Grocery*. Within minutes he called out to his wife to bring Latina inside.

When Latina thought back to it later, there wasn't much she could remember about being led into the back living quarters of the dusty old store. Her stomach was kinked in little knots and her hair felt pasted to her head. There was an old bathtub that stood up on four quaint claw legs and the pipes came out of holes in the wooden floor to the faucets. She recalled sitting on the edge of that old tub while her mother held a cold cloth to her burning forehead. Voices coming from the store drifted back to them as Latina sat there attempting to regain her composure.

An older man was saying, "I'm Orville Boles, and this here's my wife, Maude. You folks heading for the Nettleton place?"

"No," she could hear her father explain in his patient professor's voice. "We're looking for the farm that Professor Kirkland owns. He's a friend of mine. He's in Europe for the summer, so we're renting it."

"Yep. That's the one. It's the Nettleton place. The Nettleton's owned it nigh on to forty years."

When Latina emerged from the back room with her mother, Mr. Boles was drawing her father a map explaining how to get to the farm. Thin, frail Maude Boles smiled at her sympathetically and made a *tsking* sound through her dentures. Latina looked away in disdain, wishing someone would offer her a place to sit down.

It wasn't until that very moment that she noticed the young man sitting in a straight-backed chair tipped against the wall beside a pop cooler. His arms were folded across his broad chest and his long legs allowed his feet to remain flat on the floor. A shock of sandy curls lay across his forehead and his dancing blue eyes were laughing at her.

"Let's go back to the car, Mom," she whispered as her hand flew to her mussed and matted hair.

"We can wait until you're feeling better," her mother suggested. "No hurry now. We're almost at the farmhouse."

A few minutes earlier, Latina had never wanted to ride in a car again, but now she said, "Let's go the car *now*, Mother! Please!"

She couldn't bear those laughing eyes on her another second.

The screen door was held by a snaky-looking spring that banged it shut as they went out.

Her father and Dirk followed shortly, chattering about their first glimpse of Zell's Bush. "Paulie," Mr. Harmen said, "did you ever see the likes of that store? Just like a scene from Ma and Pa Kettle, wasn't it?"

"Somewhat, I suppose." Her mother's voice was noncommittal.

"That tall guy was really cool," Dirk was saying in his usual breathless way. "Did you see the muscles on that dude? What'd they say his name was, Dad?"

"Clouse. Tully Clouse, I think. They drawl so that I can barely make out their words."

Clouse! Latina seethed inwardly. Should have been Louse! That clod, who looked like he was wearing his little brother's jeans, had laughed at her! As if coming to this miserable place and then getting sick weren't degrading enough, that hillbilly had had the audacity to laugh at her!

Gray clouds filled the sky as they traveled the winding road from Boles's Grocery to the farm. Twice, their car bumped over small metal bridges that rattled beneath them in protest. Mrs. Harmen remarked that the road must wind and turn about more than the streams did.

Latina mutely agreed.

The fact that the old two-story farmhouse was in better repair than Latina thought it might be, did nothing to cheer her. It was nothing in comparison to their charming cottage at the cove on the East Coast where they had stayed every summer for as long as she could remember.

A few drops of rain had begun to fall as Mr. Harmen brought the last of their luggage into the cavernous house. After the tedious hours traveling from their home in Eagleton, Ohio, Dirk now exploded into a missile, shooting from room to room. His insatiable curiosity about the big house made it impossible for his father to get any help from him.

Dirk reported that there were four spacious bedrooms upstairs and immediately staked his claim on the southeast room that overlooked the meandering driveway and the expanse of the valley. He wanted to see the sun come up, so he loudly proclaimed as he leaned precariously over the balcony railing at the head of the stairs.

The musty smells of the old house, which had recently been opened for them by one of the local women, didn't do much for Latina's queasy stomach.

"As soon as I locate the teakettle, Latina," Mrs. Harmen said as they carried boxes into the kitchen, "I'll heat you some soup and make you a cup of tea."

Latina set her box on the kitchen table, which was spread with a worn, flower-print oilcloth, and watched her mother who was now staring around the spacious room. "This place smells like my Grandma's old farmhouse." Latina was surprised. She hadn't heard her mother speak much about her family, all of whom had lived in Kansas and had long since passed away before Latina was born.

The air was cool and clammy. As soon as Latina found the right suitcase, she pulled out her bulky blue cardigan and slipped its warmth over her bare arms. She then grabbed her transistor radio from the same suitcase and played music to chase the formidable silence out of the house.

Now raindrops pelted more persistently. Mr. Harmen planted his tall frame before a window in the front room and looked out across the wide front porch. He tamped his unlit pipe with his forefinger. "It's a bit cool," he commented. "Wonder if we could find enough dry wood to start a fire!"

The spacious room was flanked on the north by a massive stone fireplace between two bay windows.

Dirk was banging out a painful rendition of "Peter, Peter, Pumpkin Eater" on an upright piano he had discovered. Hitting a final chord, he jumped up at his father's suggestion. "All right! Lead me to the woodpile. I brought my trusty hatchet."

Latina marvelled at the two of them as they walked into the deepening rainy blackness as though it were their well-lit yard in Eagleton.

Although she knew her mother needed help in the kitchen, Latina sank into one of the overstuffed chairs in front of the fireplace and closed her eyes.

Presently, her father and Dirk brought in some sickly looking sticks of wood and made an effort to start a fire. "Jim told me about the remodeling they'd done on this place," her father was saying, his head inside the fireplace's black cavity. "He seemed to be particularly proud of this fireplace." He placed kindling on top of old newspapers. "I can see why he was proud—it's a beaut!"

Good old Professor Kirkland, Latina thought. She wished he'd never come on staff at Eagleton Community College where her father was head of the history department. That way they would never have heard of Zell's Bush, Missouri. She thought again of the awful moment at supper two weeks ago when Ross had announced to the family that they were not going to the cove this summer. Latina had nearly choked.

"Your mother and I have been discussing this off and on for some time," he told them in his slow way. "As you know, the cove has become increasingly crowded and commercialized each year. It's not the quiet summer retreat it once was. There are disco joints, pawn shops, the oceanfront park and tourist traps everywhere. I'm finding it more and more difficult to complete the research I set out to do each summer. Not enough peace and quiet."

Latina had sat there frozen as she heard about Jim Kirkland's sabbatical in Europe and his offer to rent out the quiet farm in the Ozarks. "And I've decided to take him up on the offer," her dad said with finality.

The commercialization, as her father called it, consisted of wonderful fun places to be. Especially the dinner club with a dance floor out over the sparkling water, where she and Kent Starner had danced in a dream world last summer. A few days before leaving Eagleton, she'd received a note from Kent explaining that he would be in Mexico for two weeks, at the beginning of the summer, but then would be meeting her at Periwinkle Cove in mid-June. Painfully, she wrote back to explain to him of her sudden change of plans and gave him the Zell's Bush address.

Latina turned toward what was left of the fire. She could see Dirk's initial excitement over the prospect of a glowing fire was waning. The wood they had found was too wet. "What are we going to do tonight with no television?" His voice was flat.

Latina sank further back into the chair. "Let me stay in Eagleton with Grandma Staton and get a job," she had begged her mother privately in her room after hearing her father's news. "At least I'll be with my friends all summer."

But her mother had shaken her head. "Next year you'll be graduating from high school, Latina. Let's let this be a together-summer for our family. We'll have a different kind of good time. You'll see."

Latina had seen all she wanted to see of this different kind of good time. The chill of the room permeated her very bones.

Professor Harmen leaned back on his heels. Weariness was taking the edge off his enthusiasm as well. He sighed. "It'd be best for all of us, I suppose, to go to bed early this evening. We're all exhausted from the trip."

"To bed?" Dirk's groan of disbelief was followed by a call from his mother in the kitchen.

The three of them were thankful to see the kitchen table set with thick ham sandwiches and mugs of steaming tea. Mrs. Harmen had closed off the kitchen doors and the old gas cooking stove's oven door was open, warming the room.

"Paulie," Mr. Harmen said, shaking his head. "You outsmarted these two Boy Scouts in getting your fire started." He gave his wife a grateful hug, while Dirk plowed into a sandwich.

Latina chose to sip alternately on her soup and the tea, letting the warmth trickle down to her insides.

"What a blessing," Mrs. Harmen said, "that the Kirklands called ahead to have a lady open the house for us." She rubbed her fingers across the oilcloth thoughtfully. "I think they said her name was Garwood."

"Garwood?" Dirk's interest was sparked. "I saw a sign just up from the grocery store that said, Garwood's Saw Mill. Maybe that's where the lady lives."

"I don't know, son." The professor puffed on his pipe, sending the sweet, familiar aroma into the air. "In such a small town, everyone is related to everyone. There could be fifty families of Garwoods."

"I doubt that there are fifty families in the whole town," Latina commented dryly. She hadn't meant it as a joke, but her family chuckled nonetheless.

She thought of her best friend, Camille Dawson, who was leaving for the Bahamas as soon as school was out. The two girls had talked often of the awesome tans they would have next fall as they began their senior year together at Eagleton High. The thought of Cammie lying out on the deck of the luxurious cruise ship, while she sat in the kitchen of a dank old farmhouse was unbearable. How could her parents have done this to her?

"The screened-in porch is perfect to catch the afternoon sun," her mother was saying in an irritatingly casual voice. "I think I'll put some hanging planters out there."

Her mother, who at first seemed to be Latina's only ally, was sounding terribly settled in. It was worrisome for Latina, who was now dreading going up the stairs into the darkened bedroom.

Her parents had chosen the east bedroom adjacent to Dirk's and her father had mentioned that he preferred the room overlooking the backyard for his study. The room adjoining the study was left for Latina.

The wind came up and was whistling in the windows as Latina scurried quickly into the strange bed. Her radio lay on the pillow near her ear, but the rattling windows gave stiff competition to its sound.

She fumbled with the dial on the transistor before she realized that the batteries were not fresh. Why hadn't she thought to replace them?

It was a wretched beginning to what she knew was going to be a wretched summer.

# Chapter Two

When footsteps on the creaking stairs awakened Latina the next morning, sunlight was streaming in the tall windows. Her father passed by her door carrying a box loaded with his typewriter and some books.

"Good morning, Latina," he said, pausing at her door. "We decided to let you sleep and get over your jet lag." He chuckled at his own joke.

"Thanks a bunch," she answered. His silly grin drew a reluctant smile from her.

It was comfortable to lie there and listen to the busy noises her father made in the adjoining room. In the morning light, looking down on the jade-green, freshly rain-washed backyard, she almost had to admit this was a good place for him to study. Lazyily, she got out of bed, pulled, on her robe, and headed downstairs.

Her mother was puttering in the kitchen. "This place has such a homey atmosphere, doesn't it!" she commented cheerily.

Latina's answer was a noncommittal grunt. She had several other adjectives that weren't as flattering as "homey," but obviously this wasn't the time to express them. Absently, she poured a bowl of corn flakes and considered whether to eat a piece of cold bacon.

She thought of Cammie on her way to the Bahamas this very minute. Obviously she would be staying at the most exclusive hotels. And perhaps Kent had already arrived in Mexico. Hopefully, he would write soon.

Leaving half the soggy cereal, she walked out to the screened-in porch and shivered as the rain-washed breeze touched her arms. She moved past green metal lawn chairs with chipped paint, out the screen door and down the stone steps, walking barefoot onto the wet grass.

She could hear Dirk thrashing around in the tumbledown barn off to her right. He had already discovered some rusty horseshoes and had asked his mother for permission to take them back to Eagleton. He seemed to be entranced by this so-called farm and the "swallowing-up" hills, as he had so aptly named them.

"They're swallowing us up," he had muttered as he gazed out the back car window at the ebony hills. To Latina, the thought was about as appealing as Jonah's experience in the belly of the whale. Lucky Jonah. His confinement was three short days. Hers was three eternal months.

"Want some help unpacking, dear?" Mrs. Harmen asked as Latina stood at the back door drying her wet feet on an old towel.

"Thanks," she replied dully. "I think I can handle it." Reluctantly, she retreated to her room to work.

After lunch, her father suggested driving down to Boles's to ask Mr. Boles where they could buy firewood. "If we locate some," he said, "we'll stack it on the porch so it'll be handy for cool evenings."

"Are there going to be many more cool evenings?" Latina asked.

"Well, Latina, let's face it. It won't be quite as balmy as Periwinkle Cove."

Latina thought of brilliant sunshine on sparkling white sand and pulled her cardigan more snugly around her.

"If we're going to the grocery store, I can get BBs for my gun," her brother said. Latina had hoped Boles's Grocery was "uptown" enough to have batteries for her transistor, but this turned out to be a vain hope.

Orville Boles was in no hurry to get up from his chair behind the small checkout counter. But he stretched forth a leathery hand to grasp Mr. Harmen's and gave a cheery "Howdy! What can I do for you?"

"We need some firewood, Mr. Boles, to take the edge off the nippy evenings. Know where we can get some?"

"It has been a mite cooler this spring. You might need some wood at that," the words came out of the old man as though churned out slowly by a crank.

Latina searched for the batteries. Mrs. Boles appeared from nowhere and patted her shoulder with a thin, blue-veined hand. "How are you today, dearie?"

"I'm fine, thank you," Latina answered, shrinking from her touch.

Showing the dead battery to Mrs. Boles, Latina heard Mr. Boles telling her father to check at the Garwood's Saw Mill for firewood, which he pronounced "farwood."

"We saw that sign at the turnoff," her father commented. "They have firewood, do they?"

"Nope, just lumber." Mr. Boles fell silent.

Professor Harmen waited.

Then the old man clumped his chair down on its four legs with a bang. "That young fellow you met yesterday, Tully Clouse. He works there. For a little extra money, he'll cut tops for you and carry them to you in his pickup."

Meanwhile Mrs. Boles slowly fingered through battery packages gritty with dust, looking very closely to make out the labels. After a long time, she turned to Latina. "We don't have such a one as that," she said, squinting. "Sorry."

Her father was speaking to Mr. Boles, "Thanks, Orville. We'll stop by the mill on our way home. Say,

Pauline and Dirk have a couple of items here that we need to pay for.''

"Maude!" Mr. Boles called without moving. "You gotta couple of customers."

Latina slipped the lifeless battery in her jump-suit pocket and stepped out onto the dilapidated wooden porch in front of the store. The miniature main street was, to her, like a cartoon from a joke book—a small, littered gas station, a cement-block bank building painted a dull brown, and Boles's store. Not even a pizza place, she thought wistfully. It was like coming to another country.

"Clouse did odd jobs for them other people that lived up at the Nettleton place," she could hear Mr. Boles's voice through the screen door. "He's a dandy worker!"

As she climbed into the car, Latina hoped that he wouldn't be doing any work in their house. How much worse could the summer get?

Turning off the main road at the sign, the Harmens drove a short distance before reaching the mill operation which was situated in a level clearing in a small valley.

Lurching down the rutted drive, they met a semi-trailer heavily loaded with cut lumber, grinding its gears as it slowly made its way up from the mill. Her father was forced to pull off the drive and let it pass. The driver waved and grinned. Ross returned the wave, then drove into the graveled area near another parked trailer.

As Latina got out of the car, she was greeted by the warm fragrance of cut wood and the shrill screams of the saws that were housed in open-sided sheds. Metal chains clanked harshly as workers loosened them to unload freshly cut logs from the trailer bed.

A bear of a man came striding toward Mr. Harmen with a large outstretched hand. "Howdy," he said. "I'm Parke Garwood. You folks looking for something?"

Ross introduced the family, explained where they were staying for the summer and added that Orville Boles had told them of the possibility of getting firewood at the mill.

"Clouse does that," Mr. Garwood said, pointing to the sheds. "He's right here. Let's go ask him." To Latina's mother, he said, "Why don't you womenfolk head on up to the house." He indicated a winding pathway that led to a small house tucked up against the side of the hill. "Just knock at the door. I'm of a mind Etta Ann still has some coffee hot."

It irritated Latina to be referred to as "womenfolk" and to be told what to do by this stranger. As her mother thanked him and made her way up the path, Latina deliberately held back and strolled the other way. When her mother glanced back, Latina shook her head.

She wanted no part of that house. This place reminded her of the nursey rhyme of the crooked little man with the crooked little house. How she longed for the straight, square, named streets of Eagleton!

Dirk had discovered the mountain of sawdust behind the sheds and was happily burrowing around in it. Latina had already noticed Tully working under the open shed along with several other men. His broad-shouldered frame was unmistakable. She watched as her father was introduced to the young man and she wondered if the workers were laughing at them for wanting firewood in the summer.

As she turned to walk back to the car, she noticed several hand-carved figurines on a ledge of the shed nearest her. Giving in to her curiosity, she stepped over to have a closer look. The miniature works of art were polished to a high sheen. Several were of animals— squirrels and raccoons, but one that especially interested her was of a little girl. She picked it up to study the intricate details. The girl's head was cocked to one side like a tiny bird listening for dangers in the forest.

"Well, look here." The voice startled her. "Last night's spring rain done brought a blossom to the hills."

Latina turned to look into the face of a dark-eyed young man with straight black hair.

Slowly she set the figurine back in its place.

"I'm Collier Hunsecker, and this here's my cousin, Tully Clouse," he said.

Beside him, towering nearly a head taller, stood Tully, and once again she was looking into the lively blue eyes that were twinkling in laughter at her.

"And what might your name be?" Collier asked as he filled a cup from a large metal water cooler.

"Her name is Latina," ventured Tully in an even tone. "I heard them say yesterday over at Boles's."

"Sounds purty as a flower, don't it?" Collier's admiring dark eyes looked at her over the rim of the metal cup. "Latina." He reached forward to touch her dark hair that lay over her shoulder against the bright blue of her jumpsuit. She stepped back with a sudden movement.

"When I first saw this flower," Tully put in, "a drive through the hills had rather wilted it." His drawl was less pronounced than his cousin's.

"Wilted, huh?" Collier retorted. "That little Latina-Flower? It sure came back to life, now didn't it?"

Latina was annoyed. She didn't intend to be talked about as though she were a botanical specimen. "I came back to life all right," she said. "Because I'm of the highly resistant variety!" Whirling about, she hastily retreated to the safety of the car and slammed the door on their laughter. She pretended to be reading something in her lap and was thankful they couldn't see it was a road map. She wished her parents would hurry and take her from this awful place.

Presently, a tall, slender young girl in jeans and a faded print blouse came down the path from the house. She approached smiling and motioned for Latina to roll down the window.

"Howdy," she said breathlessly. "I'm Donna Dee Garwood. I didn't know until this very minute that you were out here, or I'd have come to meet you sooner. Your mama just mentioned you were out here alone. Welcome to Zell's Bush. We're so glad to have you."

The drawl of words didn't seem so repulsive coming from this girl. Her welcome sounded genuine—a salve to Latina's wounded ego.

"I guess this place is pretty different from what you're used to, huh?" she asked kindly.

"That's an understatement." Quickly Latina added, "I guess I'm just not used to these hills—the uh, closeness of them." She was fumbling, because honestly, she didn't know for sure what it was she didn't like. It was as if hidden danger lurked in the dense trees. The thick hills were ominous and foreboding.

"You'll get used to them and love them," the girl replied. "I work in Palatka and I'm not home much, but I'd be glad to take you there next Saturday to do some shopping or just fool around some."

Latina remembered driving through Palatka. It wasn't much bigger than Zell's Bush and nothing like Eagleton, but the friendly spirit in which the invitation was offered spurred her to accept with a degree of graciousness.

As they discussed their plans, her parents came down the path followed by Mr. Garwood and his plump wife, Etta Ann.

"You should have come up to the house with your mama," Mrs. Garwood said after introductions had been made. "No need for you sitting out here like a scared rabbit. When you come back, you come on in like you're one of us. You hear?"

Latina nodded and smiled.

As they bumped out of the deeply rutted driveway, Latina marvelled at the Garwoods' congeniality. She had imagined these people would resent intruders.

Her father was talking excitedly about Mr. Garwood's aging father, known as Old Man Gar, who lived alone in the hills. Parke felt the elderly man might open his storehouse of bygone memories and tell about the original settling of Zell's Bush.

"I think I've hit upon a new research project, Paulie." Her father's voice was laced with childlike enthusiasm. "Maybe enough for a book—about these people and their ancestors and their way of life up here."

"A book?" Her mother reached over and patted his shoulder tenderly. "How wonderful, Ross. Sounds like a marvelous opportunity."

Latina was uncomfortable in the midst of all this good news. As the car careened up the hills, she attempted to peer through the thick forest, but she couldn't see past the dense trees. Somehow, she had expected the people in the town to be just as closed to her family, and was surprised to find that they weren't.

Donna Dee could very well be the salvation of her summer. Meeting her had been a respite after the run-in with those two overgrown louts.

She was certainly looking forward to Saturday.

# Chapter Three

Mr. Harmen had had the foresight to load a few logs in the trunk while at the sawmill, since Tully wouldn't make a delivery until the next day.

The orange glow of the flames in the stone fireplace that evening, accompanied by intermittent pops and snaps, transformed the dank living room.

Her father rummaged through the bookshelves that lined the west wall and found some board games and he immediately challenged Dirk to a game.

Latina was surprised to see her mother come into the room with skeins of yarn, crochet hooks and a magazine full of patterns. Her mother hadn't done handiwork for years and had said she didn't care about it any more. Actually, she had had little free time since she'd gone back to teaching freshman composition at Eagleton Community College this past year.

Latina watched her mother's peaceful face as the crochet hook threaded in and out, carrying with it the trail of variegated pastels of yarn. Everyone seemed so disgustingly contented!

Restlessly, Latina stepped to the bay windows, which were recessed with padded window seats on either side of the fireplace. There were no streetlights, no yard lights, no house lights, no hint of any other living thing on the other side of the glass. Only her sad reflection staring back at her.

In their letters through the winter, she and Kent had talked of this being the best summer of their entire lives. When he'd first noticed her last year, it had been like a dream come true. They'd met at the drugstore, which was the hangout for all the kids who regularly spent summers at the Cove. Soon Kent was coming by the cottage nearly every day to take her swimming, picnicking, yachting on his father's boat, or dancing in the evenings. There had been an air of assuredness about him so lacking in other guys she'd met. Tall, tan and very blond, Kent always turned heads in a crowd. Sometimes they went off from the others and walked down the beach hand-in-hand, out to the rugged, rocky point. It became a special place for them. It was there, at the point, where he first held her close and told her he loved her.

Perhaps her parents had come here because they thought she was too serious about Kent. The recurring thought gnawed at her. If that was true, they were making a terrible mistake. She'd never forget Kent. Never! And she was sure he would be coming to visit her on his way back from Mexico. Then everyone would see how vital it was for them to be together.

She turned from her reflection in the window to the bookshelves. Professor Kirkland had stocked them well. She paged through a couple of volumes before settling on a mystery. She planned to lose herself in the book.

The plot was mediocre at best, and Latina hadn't realized until she was nearly half-finished that it was having a morbid effect on her. Later, after everyone had settled in for the night, the silence in her room became more oppressive than before. Branches scratched against the windows and the wind whipped the clouds past the moon. She stifled her fears, half hoping her mother might come to quell them. But no one came.

When the morning sun streamed in her window, Latina sat upright and shook off the moroseness of the previous evening. She jumped out of bed, reached for her robe, and ran down to the kitchen. Grabbing the bacon from the battered old refrigerator, she laid strips in the cast-iron skillet. The clatter of setting the table and the cooking smells soon woke the family.

Within the hour, they were chatting amiably around the table, teasing Latina, asking why she hadn't gotten up earlier and why she hadn't fixed at least a dozen more fried eggs. She laughed along with her father and brother, determined that she would find something constructive to do. She couldn't simply sit and rot.

Her father and Dirk announced that they were taking a hike through the valley toward Zell's Bush. Her mother said perhaps on another day she would join them, but she wasn't settled in enough to go running off. Visions of snakes, lizards and scorpions slithering under the rocks and dead logs prompted Latina's refusal of their invitation.

Later, as she moved about the old house, she envisioned the Kirkland children running about playing games of tag and make believe. Before Kent had come into her life, she too could have been swept up in the novelty of such an out-of-the-way place. But he had changed the way she looked at everything around her, and now Zell's Bush just looked like any other boring hick town.

By midmorning, all her good intentions had drained away. Listlessly, she followed the sounds of hammering out in the kitchen where her mother was perched on a stool hanging wall plaques. Dutifully, Latina offered assistance. As she handed up the hammer or nails when asked, her mind floated away again to where the kids at Periwinkle Cove would be shouting as they ran into the foamy breakers, or as they tanned themselves in the hot sun.

"Latina? You asleep?"

"Huh?"

"I said, will you please go down to the road and get the mail? I thought I heard the mailman's car go by."

"Sorry, I guess I was lost in thought. Sure," she said, laying the hammer on the table, "I'll go."

"And what choice do I have?" she mumbled as she pushed the front door open. "The highlight of my day—to take a trip down the driveway to the mailbox."

As she returned from the dusty mailbox, carrying the few pieces of unimportant mail forwarded from Eagleton, she heard the rattle of an approaching vehicle. Not many people traveled this road. It slowed at the end of the drive and turned in. Glancing over her shoulder, she saw a battered blue pickup coming up the drive. It was Tully delivering the wood. As she stepped from the gravel drive into the grass, the pickup stopped beside her.

"Ride to the house?" he called over the noise of the clattering motor.

"I need the exercise, thank you." Her words were clipped.

"Suit yourself." He gave a nod and a half-smile, shifted the gears and drove on. Little rocks spit out from the tires, hitting her bare legs. She glowered at the pickup as it moved behind the house where the wood was to be stacked inside the screened-in porch.

How much wood could they need for cool evenings? At Periwinkle Cove, she would have been in her bikini. She shivered as she walked beneath the cool shade of the towering oaks.

Placing the mail on the piano in the front room, she glanced through the bookshelves again. Oh, for a boring television rerun, or something! Anything! Noises from the kitchen indicated her mother was still puttering. How could her mother enjoy such a decrepit kitchen that was so paltry in comparison to their own back home?

"Latina? Come here a minute," she heard her mother call.

"Here." Mrs. Harmen thrust a tall glass of ice water at her as she slowly entered the kitchen. "Take this to our hard-working young man out there." She pointed to where Tully was bringing in armloads of wood as though they were toothpicks.

Why doesn't she hand it to him herself, Latina thought. Through the door, she watched Tully work. Each move was calculated and measured. His thick, sandy-brown hair fell carelessly across his forehead.

As she opened the screen door leading from the kitchen, he turned toward her and flashed a wide smile. "Howdy," he said.

"Mother thought you looked hot and thirsty," she said lamely. "She asked me to bring this out." It sounded redundant. Almost childish.

"I'm obliged to your mother. She's mighty thoughtful." Amusement shone in his eyes.

He's laughing at me again, she thought. Why did this country bumpkin continually put her on the defensive? She turned to go.

"Say, there's a little wood tick there on your leg," he said softly. His voice had a husky quality about it.

He was probably kidding. She'd play it cool and not look down or panic.

"I can get it off for you real simple."

Still she stood there wondering how to best call his bluff.

"If you pull it off and leave the head in, it could give you some bad trouble," he continued in the same soft, husky tone.

A gasp escaped from her when she looked down at the tiny creature buried in her skin just above the knee. How she detested crawling things! She restrained a scream.

He stepped toward her and placed his large hands on her arms and gently seated her in the metal lawn chair nearest her. She felt the icy metal touch the backs of her legs.

He knelt down before her on the gray floor. His sandy hair was very close to her face. She felt she couldn't breathe.

Deftly, he grasped the miniscule insect in the tips of his fingernails and turned it around. Once it slipped, and he patiently turned it around again, "clockwise," he explained, "so they'll let go." He looked up momentarily and she was looking full into his clear blue eyes.

She wanted to push him away. It was all his fault! If he hadn't run her off the driveway into the grass, she wouldn't even have had a tick on her leg.

"This won't be the last of these pesky fellows you'll meet up with," he said. "Just remember to turn them clockwise and they'll let loose." As he said the words, the insect released itself into his fingers.

"Want to see him?"

She recoiled. "Get it away from me." Her voice was sharp.

He pinched it between his fingers and calmly rose and dropped it outside the door on the grass.

"I guess I should thank you," she said coolly, struggling for self-possession.

"Mercy no, ma'am," he retorted. "I'm used to it. I pick them off my hound dog all the time and she never says thank you." He was out the door now ready to leave. He leaned his back through the door a moment and said with a grin, "She does lick my hand, though!" The screen door slammed.

Latina's face was burning as she whirled about and hurried into the house. The blue pickup laughed its rattle all the way back down the driveway.

Latina leaned against the rusty bridge railing and absently dribbled tiny pebbles through her fingers to the stream below. A swift bubbling current disguised the effects of the falling pebbles as though they'd never been dropped.

If only it were as easy to erase the harsh words she'd exchanged with her mother a few moments earlier. But the words, and the slamming of the front door as she ran out, still echoed in her ears.

It was Friday, and through the long boring week her father had spent contented hours in his study and Dirk incessantly roamed about the woods in search of new discoveries. The men of the family were already deliriously happy with the summer arrangements, and her mother was becoming more so each day.

Yesterday, her mother had found some potted plants at a roadside stand, and this morning she had set about to pot them in hanging planters. When she'd asked Latina to lend a hand, it had been the last straw!

"What an absolute gas!" she said. "Spending my summer playing with potted plants!"

In restrained tones, her mother'd remarked that Latina could find something to keep her occupied if she tried.

"I'd have to try all right," Latina had answered bitterly. "For the crime of being an active, fun-loving teenager, I've been banished into exile in this backwoods, no-man's land, and now my punishment is to find something to do here!"

She'd fled from the house and charged up the road in a direction she'd never yet been. How, she asked in bewilderment, could her parents be so unfeeling? Of course, she loved them. Among all her friends, she felt she had the best parents, and even now she wanted to please them. But visions of Periwinkle Cove tormented her as she compared it to this place.

And then there was Tully Clouse. His appearance at the house last evening to help her father dig postholes sent her hurrying to her room. After he and her father had worked a while in the cool dusky evening, she'd heard him playing on his harmonica. The tunes that floated up into her partially opened window had irritated her as much as his laughing eyes. She'd closed the window and thought he looked up at her from where he was perched on the tailgate of his old blue pickup. She'd stayed away from the window after that.

He lived up this road somewhere. She knew, because every day his pickup rumbled by in a cloud of dust from this direction. It wouldn't have surprised Latina if this dusty little road simply wound around up this hill and disappeared into the side of the mountain. It was that kind of country—strange—with strange people inhabiting it.

At the edge of the stream beneath the bridge, Latina noticed sunlight reflecting off a metallic object. She looked for a way down to the streambed. At the edge of the bridge, she found a slightly obscured pathway through the underbrush to the water's edge. The stream was narrow, with pebbled banks spreading out on either side.

Precariously, she made her way down the path only to discover the object wasn't metal at all, but a small rock glistening in the light that filtered through dense trees. She stuffed it in her pants pocket for Dirk.

Picking her way cautiously along the stream, she looked for other interesting rocks for her brother. Presently, the water widened into a faster current. She pulled off her tennis shoes and waded ankle-deep. Each step in the cold water made her catch her breath. This clear water no doubt came from the underground caves her father had told her about. Glancing behind her, she could see nothing except the stream and trees.

A series of gentle falls forced her to step out of the water and onto the bank. She put her shoes on and made her way easily through the trees, up the incline and then back toward the water again.

There she saw a mirrored pool of azure water surrounded by willows. Directly across the pool, rising up out of the undergrowth and half smothered by ivy, was a deserted mill. Its mammoth waterwheel, still intact, was poised above its wavering image in the water.

To her left was a vast stone overhang. She moved toward it and sat down on the flat rocks beneath. It was like a cave. She could sit upright and not touch her head on the damp rocks above.

Studying the scene before her, she decided she would like to paint it. What a challenge! The little paintings she had done in the past had been admired by her parents. They had encouraged her to pursue her talent. But there had never been a moment to spare. Her mother purchased supplies for her last summer, but Latina had laid them aside, ignoring the special craggy cliff at Periwinkle Cove that had begged to be painted.

Kent would love this place, she told herself smiling, just as they had loved the ocean together. If he should decide to come miles out of his way to see her, now she would have something to share with him. They would come here and spend the afternoons together.

But did he care enough to come? He'd cared enough to write last winter, surely that proved something! She dared not admit to herself that there weren't nearly as many letters to her as she had mailed to him.

A rustle on the rocky ledge above startled her from her thoughts. She froze as a small greenish-brown lizard slithered down the damp surface toward her. It stopped close to her, blinking like a tiny prehistoric monster. She reached for a rock to throw and her movement sent him gliding away.

For all its beauty this wasn't a very safe place to be. Distressing thoughts of rattlesnakes haunted her as she set out for home. She was glad when she reached the safety of the road.

# Chapter Four

The car windows were rolled down and the fragrant breeze blew in on her hair. Latina usually despised having her hair windblown, but when driving with Donna Dee, for some reason, it didn't seem to matter.

Her new friend was discussing her secretarial position at the Palatka law firm. "No one was as shocked as I was when I landed the job. Kids in the consolidated high school look down on us kids from Zell's Bush as if we aren't quite up to snuff. But when I was at business school, I studied extra hard to prove them wrong—and I did it!" Her short curls bobbed as she spoke. "I know a proudful look isn't becoming, but when my old school chums walk past the office and there I am at the front desk of Jenner, Jenner and Sons, I feel like the tall hog at the trough.''

Latina laughed. She wanted to relate to that feeling of accomplishment, but she could think of few things in her life of which she could be justifiably proud. It was a disturbing thought.

Donna Dee parked the car near Palatka's massive stone courthouse and they strolled across the square to Larsen's Drug Store. They sat in a front booth near the windows in full view of the oak-shaded courthouse square.

"It's my shorthand I'm struggling with," Donna Dee admitted. "I still get skitterish when those nice lawyers start dictating to me, and I know I could do better."

"What you need is someone to dictate practice letters to you," Latina suggested. "There's a typing workbook in the bookcase at the house that has business letters in it. How would it be if we got together some evening and I dictated to you?"

"Oh, would you mind, Latina? I know it would help so much. It's right nice of you to offer."

They ordered Cokes and Donna Dee introduced Latina to the waitress and to several other young people seated in the adjoining booths. Their easy conversation and good-natured ribbing could easily have been coming from Wally's Grill near her school in Eagleton.

Returning to their own conversation, Donna Dee said with a knowing smile, "I bet you didn't spend your evenings back home dictating business letters."

She wanted to cry, "You're right! Especially in the summer!" but she pushed the thought aside. "No matter. I'd love to help you. Besides, I might have to take shorthand next year myself. Mother says it'll help in taking notes at college."

"You're going to college?"

"My parents both teach at our local college." Latina stirred the ice in her cup with the straw. "I suppose I'd be a family disgrace if I didn't go."

Donna Dee's green eyes were wide. "You're so blessed. What will you study?"

Latina twisted a strand of dark hair around her forefinger. Her mother often asked the same question. "Plan your high-school subjects to fit in with your major," she'd say. But for the life of her, Latina had no idea what her life goals were.

She chose to turn aside the question with, "I'm not sure yet," and changed the subject. "Is there a paint shop in Pakatka? I'd like to buy some paints and canvases and try my hand at a scene I saw yesterday."

Donna Dee nodded. "The Hobby House is just down the street from the Jenner law office. Scads of tourists come through here who need art supplies. They're drawn to our hills. You an artist?"

"I've dabbled at it," she answered carefully. "My folks think I'm good, but you know how parents are."

Later at the Hobby House, Latina not only found her supplies, but also a wooden carrying case in which she could cart everything to the millpond. She also purchased three packages of batteries for her transistor. If she were in for the duration, she might just as well gear up for survival.

On their way back to the car, Donna Dee took her by the office of Jenner, Jenner and Sons. They were peering in the window through cupped hands like children at a toy shop when a voice spoke from behind them.

"Shopping?"

As they whirled about, Donna Dee nearly stumbled over Latina's wooden case at her feet. "Oh, Mr. Jenner," she gasped. "I didn't think anyone'd be anywhere near the office on Saturday."

The casually dressed young man was visibly amused as his secretary regained her composure. When she had caught her breath, Donna Dee introduced Latina to the youngest member of the firm, Brad Jenner.

"Welcome to the Ozarks, Miss Harmen," Brad said, giving her a firm handshake. "I see you're planning to take some of our fair land home with you." He indicated the paint case on the sidewalk.

"I'm attempting to, anyway," she said with a polite smile.

"Well, we must be going about our business," Donna Dee said, helping Latina with her case. "It was a pleasure seeing you, Mr. Jenner. See you Monday."

When they neared the Zell's Bush turnoff, Latina was surprised to find the trip home was so brief, unlike the endless drive the day they'd arrived. The two girls had talked nonstop the entire way.

"What was it you found to paint, Latina?" Donna Dee asked as they crossed the rattling bridges past the sawmill.

"I went for a walk yesterday along the stream and came upon an old millpond. I'm going to try my hand with that."

"The old mill? Well, I never!" She sounded surprised.

"What is it?" Latina asked.

"I'd never have guessed you'd get that far off the road."

Latina swallowed hard over this referral to her citified ways.

"I'm sorry, Latina," Donna Dee said quickly. "I didn't mean to be rude. I'm glad you found the millpond, it's a pretty place. Before I started working, I used to go there myself and just sit. I'd be happy to see your pictures when you finish."

As they were unloading Latina's purchases at the house, Donna Dee added as an afterthought, "I think you ought to know, Latina, that Collier Hunsecker sometimes sets traps in the valley down from the millpond. He's bent on trapping year-round even though it's against the law. Just keep your eyes open when you're in the brush. They're pretty easy to spot."

"If it's against the law, why doesn't someone turn him in?"

"Collier? Oh honey, Zell's Bush is used to Collier. We just put up with him. He's got a mad on all the time. If someone turned him in and he got caught, he'd just have more to be mad about. He's awful bull-headed, that Collier is."

Latina was irritated. Now there was yet another fear to overcome if she were to return to her rendezvous spot and record it on canvas; steel traps set beneath the damp layers of rotting leaves on the forest floor. She wondered if the risk was worth it.

The screams of the big saws pierced the night air as Latina turned into the drive of Garwood's Saw Mill. It was the night she and Donna Dee had set aside to work together. Latina had thought that surely by this time the men would have finished and gone home. She lifted her hair off her collar, wishing she had tied it up off her neck. The days were beginning to get sticky.

Grabbing her typing book from the car seat, she stepped quickly across the graveled area. Under the shed, only Tully, Collier and one other man were working at the saws. They must be finishing up some special work, she thought. She'd hurry on before they saw her.

Tully was feeding a large plank of lumber through the saw to make what looked to be a small cut. Latina was at the point where the hard-packed dirt path turned to the left toward the sheds, when out of the corner of her eye, she noticed Collier moving up behind Tully. Purposely, the boy knocked against the smooth plank of precision-cut lumber causing the saw to scream and tear jaggedly into the wood.

Latina stopped dead still. Mr. Garwood appeared out of nowhere, his face livid.

"That's gonna cost you, Clouse. That's not a nail file you're working with!"

Collier had slipped away and was nonchalantly looking over a pile of scraps nearby.

Latina regarded the scene with disgust. Parke Garwood needed to know the truth. Abruptly, she turned in their direction as Tully was calmly, respectfully apologizing to him.

"My fault, sir," he said. "It slipped. I won't let it happen again."

"You can bet on that. Another expensive slip like that and I'll see to it you won't have a chance to do it again."

Mr. Garwood's back was toward her. As he leaned over to inspect the cut, Tully happened to glance up and see her. Without a word, his clear eyes signaled to her not to interfere.

She hesitated, puzzled. It wasn't right to let Collier get away with such a malicious act! She pressed her lips together and slowed her steps. She needn't bow to Tully's wishes. She could certainly tell Mr. Garwood anything she pleased!

Collier turned from the scrap pile. Spying her, he said loudly, "My, my. Here's our quick-blooming Latina-Flower."

Mr. Garwood turned to look at her. "Evening, Miss Harmen. Donna Dee's up at the house," he said, as if to let her know she had no business in the sheds.

She groped for words. "My father wanted me to be sure to remind Tully we'll be needing him to help out up at our place tomorrow when he's off work," she said awkwardly. Her eyes went from Mr. Garwood's lined face to Tully's young one.

"Thanks," Tully said, his eyes meeting hers.

Deliberately, Latina forced her legs into measured steps up the winding path, restraining the urge to run. Well, she told herself, that should teach her something about butting into other people's affairs! Whether Tully was afraid of his weird cousin, or even threatened by him, it was definitely none of her business. She was quite breathless as she approached the Garwood's front door.

Mrs. Garwood met her with a hug and led her to where Donna Dee was waiting. She stepped into a living room dominated by a squat, black wood-burning stove. The wallpaper, the linoleum, the braided rug, and even the divan- and chair-throws were of many colors and patterns, seemingly purchased, or acquired arbitrarily, for service only. There was an unmistakable warmth that appealed to Latina. She felt instantly at home.

Donna Dee was eager to work on her shorthand. They spread their books and papers out on the dining-room table as Latina dictated letter after letter.

By the end of the evening, Donna Dee was whipping out the swirled characters as fast as Latina could dictate.

"I don't think it's your shorthand that's the problem, Donna Dee," Latina said teasingly. "Perhaps it's the effect of the handsome young attorney who does the dictating."

"It's more likely the effect of his daddy," Donna Dee said. "That man is as mean as an old setting hen."

Before Latina left, Etta Ann offered them a snack of warm cornbread topped with syrup. Latina tried to imagine her reaction if her mother had offered her friends a snack of cornbread. With a twinge of shame, she admitted that she would have been mortified.


Several days later, Latina packed her paints and walked to the millpond. Her parents had announced they were going to a nearby lake to fish for the afternoon. Dirk immediately began to noisily sort through his tackle box on the back porch.

"I think I'll stay behind," Latina told them. Noticing her mother's look of disappointment, she added, "I hate to fish, and I thought I'd get started on some painting today."

"Sounds fine," her mother said, obviously relieved that her daughter had finally found something to do. "But remember, we may not be back until after dark."

The little hill stream had swollen since Latina's first visit, due to recent night rains. The day was warm, and steamy heat rose from the damp earth giving off a rich, fresh smell. There were fewer places to walk in the pebbled stream now. Empty-handed, she could have waded, but the case made it awkward, so she walked along the bank through thick branches that lashed her cheeks and briars that prickled through her jeans.

When she thought of Collier's steel traps, she wanted to turn and run, but the gurgling of the waterfalls told her the mill was near.

Balancing her paint box, she made her way through the trees to the smooth rock precipice beneath the jutting rock overhang. Everything was just as it had been the day she'd discovered it. Spreading out an old blanket she'd brought along, she settled down with sketchbooks and pencils.

"It's simply too beautiful," she whispered aloud. Could she ever capture the veil of mist that hung in the air near the overhang? "A false start is better than no start at all," her father used to tell her. Well, she would start!

The air was still and warm even in the recesses of the overhang. Perspiration trickled beneath her light cotton blouse, but she hardly noticed. She'd planned to stop and eat the sandwich she'd packed, but found herself holding the sandwich in her left hand while continuing to place finishing touches here and there on the sketches.

She hadn't noticed the tops of the trees stirring with the first movings of cooler air that had arrived to clash head-on with the pocket of muggy, warm air. Not having been reared in the hills, she was ignorant of the significance of these events. Up until now, she had experienced only the gentle rains, not a full-flung violent storm.

Enclosed in the thick woods and sheltered beneath the overhang, she could not see the thick boiling clouds moving in. By the time she felt the first rush of cooler air, fat raindrops were plopping into the water.

"No matter," she assured herself. "I can easily wait out a little rainstorm."

Stubbornly, she continued to sketch, confident it would soon cease. But it did not cease, nor did it let up once the torrents began to fall. She smoothed ringlets from her face and peered up through the trees. Then she gathered her supplies into the case. "It'll be over in a minute. There's no sense in getting soaked. I can wait," she told herself.

The hills echoed with violent groaning winds as a bolt of lightning flashed across the sky, followed by a roll of thunder.

Latina drew the blanket around her and cowered beneath the ledge. She couldn't bear to think that she might be trapped here all night. She placed her paint case far back where the rock formations met in a crevice. Better for it to be left behind than be ruined as she returned home. The water was steadily rising.

Now it was swiftly rushing over the lower part of the ledge where she had been sitting. Quickly, she pulled the blanket tightly around her and rushed out into the storm, hoping she could make it to the road safely.

She fought against the branches and tangling vines. The driving rain made any progress, even a few feet, a vain struggle. She'd intended to follow the streambed, but the stream wasn't in its bed. After stepping calf-deep in the overflow, she was forced to follow at a distance.

After what seemed to be an eternity of fighting, Latina sensed the undergrowth was thinning into a clearing. Surely this was the road! Now it would be a simple matter to run down the muddy track toward home. Her parents would be worried by this time.

She stared in disbelief through the silver sheets of rain at the mill on the opposite bank. She had walked in a circle! Her fears became reality—the hills had swallowed her!

It was because of the noise of the storm that she ignored the first cries of her name. It was impossible! No one knew she was here! She heard it from across the rushing water of the stream. She strained her eyes to make out the form.

It looked like...but it couldn't be—Tully!

# Chapter Five

Tully was calling and waving his arms over his head on the far bank of the rushing stream.

"The rocks!" she could hear him calling. "Below the bend. Cross there!"

Cross? Why? All she wanted was to get to the road and then on home. It was growing darker every moment. She plunged on forward.

She caught glimpses of Tully's red plaid shirt moving through the trees as he ran on ahead. When she reached the bend where the large boulders protruded from the water, he was there calling for her to cross over. She pulled the soaked blanket tighter around her.

Barely had she taken ten more steps when she felt his hands firm on her shoulders.

"Latina," he shouted, straining to make himself heard over the deluge. "My house is just the other side of that ridge." He waved a hand in the direction from which he'd come. "I'll help you cross. You can rest and get dry there."

Latina pulled away and stumbled backward. "I've got to get home! My parents don't know where I am! Please, get me to the road. Please!"

He reached for her arm, but she pulled back again.

"Latina," he shouted, "listen to me. It's three times as far to your place as mine. There could be flash-flooding at the bridges. You might not even make it to the road."

He stepped toward her. Grabbing the edges of the blanket, he secured it about her. He swept her into his arms, pressing her against him. "I can't just leave you out here in this mess."

Latina struggled to get loose.

"You'd better quit that mule-kicking, or you'll land us both in the creek," he warned her.

Latina couldn't bear to look as he stepped upon the slippery rocks across the swollen stream with her in his arms. She buried her face in his chest. Safely on the opposite bank, he strode with her in his arms, over the hill, across the gully and halfway up the next hill to his house.

"We're almost there," he said.

His boots made a thudding noise as he tramped up the wooden steps. He threw the door open and set Latina down.

Squatting in front of a wood-burning heating stove was a diminutive lady dressed in faded jeans and a boyish-looking flannel shirt. "Land sakes, Tully," she said, jumping up from where she'd been stoking the fire. "A body never knows what you'll be carrying home next, do they?"

"Mama," Tully said, "this is Latina Harmen. Her family's staying at the Nettleton place."

"The ones you've been working for? Well, well. Pleased to meet you, child. I'm Jayleen. Got caught in a bad one, didn't you?" She stepped toward Latina and surprised her with an unrestrained hug. "We must get you out of these wet things."

Latina was painfully aware of the growing puddles of rainwater spreading at her feet on the blue-flowered linoleum.

Jayleen stepped back and sized up her guest. "I think I have some britches and a shirt that'll fit you." Over her shoulder, she added, "Althea's asleep on my bed, so you'll have to change in Tully's room. Come on now before you catch your death."

"My folks," Latina said, the concern still foremost in her mind.

"Sorry, dear, but we don't have a telephone," Jayleen answered. "Perhaps Tully can drive down to check the bridges later. I doubt if you can cross tonight." Jayleen ushered her through a small living room and into Tully's bedroom.

Within minutes, Latina had changed into a large pair of jeans and a shirt that was faded but clean.

She rubbed at her matted hair with the towel Jayleen had given her and studied the room with interest. A rustic set of bookshelves were filled with volumes of poetry, a number of the classics, and Sandburg's complete works of *Lincoln*. Beneath the shelves, an unsteady card table provided a makeshift desk.

Lying face down and open on the table was a book of poetry. Latina picked it up, and saw that it was open to Tennyson's "Flower in the Crannied Wall." She scanned the short verse:

Flower in the crannied wall, I pluck you out of the crannies, I hold you here, root and all, in my hand, Little flower—but if I could understand What you are, root and all, and all in all, I should know what God and man is.

Latina couldn't connect the long-legged boy propped back in a chair at Boles's Grocery with a young man living in a bedroom like this. Each item in the room was in place, unlike Dirk's disaster at home. She had thought all guys lived in utter confusion, stuffing half their belongings under the bed.

On a whatnot above the bed were several wooden carvings like the ones she'd seen at the sawmill. She picked up a little squirrel, turning it over in her hands.

A knock at the door prompted her to replace the little figurine on the shelf. "Dinner's ready, Latina," Jayleen called.

"I'm coming. Thank you." She wrapped her wet things in the blanket and walked out into the kitchen. Tully was seated by the stove.

She smiled sheepishly. "You can have your room now. Sorry I took so long." She paused. "And I'm sorry I gave you such a bad time out there." She was uncomfortably aware of her bedraggled appearance.

"Don't give it another thought." Tully grinned.

"That storm take you by surprise?" Jayleen asked.

"Yes, ma'am. I've never seen a storm come that fast, and I was so far from home. I tried to wait it out, but when the water began to rise, I panicked."

"I've lived around here all my life, but I still get jumpy when a storm's brewing," Jayleen said.

Tully appeared in dry clothes. "What me to wake Althea?" he asked Jayleen, as he effortlessly lifted the pot of stew from her hands and set it on the table.

"Please, Tully. She can eat with us and get to know Latina."

He disappeared into the only other bedroom in the small house and returned with a thin little girl in his arms. Her head was cocked like a fragile bird's.

Latina was astonished. The figurine at the sawmill! It had been carved in the likeness of this girl. The small-boned child labored to lift her head and focus her eyes to see the stranger.

Latina had, on one other occasion, been around a child with a similar affliction. Her Scout troop had visited a learning center for handicapped children when she was in grade school. Although the other girls in the troop were repulsed, Latina had been drawn by an unspeakable compassion that she'd expressed to no one.

"Althea," Tully's voice said gently. "This is Latina. She's come to visit us."

"Hi, Althea," Latina said. "I'm very glad to meet you."

There was a moment of silence. The wood stove gave off its friendly popping noises.

Althea strained to lift her head straight. "Ah-teen-a," she pronounced slowly.

Jayleen applauded. "Wonderful Althea. You did great!"

Tully set her down on a chair where Jayleen firmly tied her in with a dish towel. Latina could see there was no other way the child could remain upright. Jayleen and Tully took turns helping her to eat.

After supper, Tully excused himself to go out and check on the chicken pens. In his absence, Latina asked Jayleen about the books in his room.

"Isn't that a sight?" Jayleen said with pride in her voice. "The other professor that was here last year took a liking to Tully and gave him several. Others, he's just collected along the way. I guess since he loves them so much, he has a way of finding them. In old bookstores and the like."

Latina took a towel from a shelf and wiped the dishes as Jayleen washed. "Where does Tully go to school?" she asked.

"He doesn't go now." Jayleen's expression was sad. "He was tops in his junior class at the valley school, but that was the year we learned we could get a tutor for Althea. After that, Tully quit school to work full-time to provide the money for Althea's tutor. Since his daddy died, Tully's really stepped in to take over.

"Well-meaning folks told us to put Althea in a home somewhere. Then I could get a job and Tully could finish school." Absently, Jayleen let her soapy hands hang limply over the sink as she spoke. "It was a hard decision to make. But Tully was dead set on keeping Althea right here. 'Can't nobody love her like we can, Mama,' he says. I agreed, but it broke my heart when he quit school. He would have graduated last month when he turned eighteen. All his life he's dreamed of going to college, but now that dream seems dim and far away."

Latina could see it was a dead-end street for Tully to continue at the sawmill with no education. There was no future for him there....

When Tully returned, he found Latina playing on the floor with Althea. He flashed her a smile of appreciation. "I took a run down to the bridge," he told them, as he hung his rain slicker on a hook near the back door. "There's flash-flooding in the valley. Can't hardly see the first bridge at all."

"Guess everyone's safe on high ground." Jayleen looked up from the jeans she was mending.

"No way you can get home tonight, Latina," Tully told her. "I'll bed down in front of the stove and you can have my room."

"Oh no, really," Latina protested. "I couldn't take your bed. I'll just take the couch here. It'll be fine."

Tully's eyes twinkled and she wondered if he were laughing at her again. "The couch it is," he said.

It was a surprise to Latina that as she settled under the soft quilts, she felt wrapped in a peace that she hadn't felt since leaving her own room in Eagleton.

The next morning, as they finished a hearty breakfast of biscuits and ham, Tully invited Latina to help him feed the livestock.

"Would Althea like to come?" she asked.

Althea picked up on it immediately. She was excited to see the "chi-chi's," which Latina was informed meant chickens.

It was apparent that Tully and Jayleen had spent endless hours teaching this girl to be independent. Althea walked with a rolling gait, with her head cocked, but her infectious joy bubbled forth continuously.

Latina helped Althea down the porch steps as Tully led the way across the wet yard and past a large washtub filled with new petunia plants. A liver-colored coon hound moseyed toward them, her tail beating out an excited welcome.

"This the hound dog with the ticks?" she asked, petting the velvet ears.

"That's her. Latina, meet Rosie. Rosie, Latina."

Rosie politely sat at Latina's feet and offered a muddy paw, which Latina shook. "My, such manners."

"It's the environment," Tully said. "High-class place here."

She blushed. Had he guessed her thoughts about Zell's Bush?

After feeding the flock of cackling chickens, he took her into a small wooden building filled with cages holding a few raccoons, squirrels, rabbits and one badger, some with splints on their legs.

"What's this?" she asked. "Your own zoo?"

"Sort of a way station," he explained as he changed the water dishes in each cage. "I help them till they can help themselves again."

Althea wiggled her fingers in a rabbit's cage and giggled as she touched the fur.

"Are these victims of your cousin's illegal trapping activities?" Latina asked.

"How did you learn about Collier?"

"Donna Dee. She warned me about the traps, just in case."

"That's what I was doing before the storm hit—checking the traps. I saw you with your sketchbook at the millpond, so later I thought I'd better go back and check on you."

She felt her face coloring. She'd been watched without even realizing it.

"And by the way," he continued, "thanks for keeping quiet about Collier knocking that plank into the saw the other night."

"Don't mention it. If you want to let him get away with murder, it's none of my concern." Every time she thought about Collier, she became angry. "Is he responsible for all this damange?" She gave a sweep of her arm.

Tully nodded. "I find them in the traps. If they're alive I nurse them back to health and then let them go."

Latina wanted to ask why Tully didn't stop Collier, but thought better of it. "Dirk would love this place," she said instead. "He's crazy about animals."

"Is he? You'll have to bring him for a visit sometime."

"I'd like that."

By afternoon, the waters had receded enough for Tully and Latina to cross the bridge and drive to her house. Her family had just arrived and had no idea she'd been gone the entire night. They too had been unable to get home and had spent the night at the Boles's.

"Seems to me we'd better have a phone installed," Latina's father said at supper that evening. "The lack of communication around this community is gosh-awful. Especially when you're cut off on all sides by rushing water."

Latina was jubilant. Now she could give the number to Kent when she wrote again. If the flood was to blame, then she was even thankful for the flood.

"Did you know," Latina asked, "that Tully has a little handicapped sister?" She described Althea's handicap. She explained how Jayleen and Tully had diligently taught her, and how Tully had quit school to work and provide funds for the tutor.

"Has he ever thought of taking correspondence courses?" Mrs. Harmen asked, her professional instinct piqued.

"I don't know," Latina answered. "He never mentioned it."

Why hadn't she thought of that? It seemed the perfect answer. But what if there wasn't enough money even for that? And how could she suggest it? He might think her an interfering busybody.

"I could help him get started," Mrs. Harmen said. "I wonder what kind of student he is."

# Chapter Six

Latina carefully picked her way along the streambed, now so placid after the turmoil of the past week. When she reached the millpond, she found to her delight that, just as she had hoped, her paints were still safe and dry by the rock ledge. She sat down and was soon lost in her painting.

By late afternoon she was ready to leave. She had just emerged from the underbrush and was walking on the road when she saw the old blue pickup rattle by with Tully at the wheel and Donna Dee beside him. Somehow, she'd never thought of them as a couple, but now it occurred to her. She pushed the thought out of her mind and continued walking home.

A letter from Kent was waiting for her on the kitchen table. She tore it open and read:

Dear Latina:

Mexico is a blast! I'll be flying into Springfield on Saturday and will rent wheels. Send me a map so that I can find my way to the majestic city of Zell's Bush.

Love, Kent

Kent was coming! She could hardly wait! Latina rushed outside so that she would see her family as soon as they returned from their fishing excursion and give them the news. Her parents had never really accepted Kent. Not that they had ever said anything unkind. On the contrary, they were almost too nice, but she could tell how they really felt.

Dirk had never been subtle about expressing his feelings. "Yuck," he said, screwing up his face in disgust when he heard the news of Kent's impending visit. "Just when we were beginning to have fun, that snob has to come and remind us how the other half lives."

Later that evening, Latina sat by her bedroom window composing her reply to Kent. Below her, she could hear Tully and her dad laughing and talking as they mended the fence in the side yard. When she had finished her brief note, she included a rough map and placed the two sheets in an airmail envelope to be mailed the following morning.

She decided to go down and talk to Tully about the correspondence course, assuming that her dad had not already mentioned it.

She found him sitting on the tailgate of his pickup. The melody from his harmonica had reached her before she came around the corner of the house. He caught sight of her and stopped in the middle of the tune, lowering the harmonica to give her a slow smile.

She hesitated, then stepped to the side of the truck, resting her arms on the cool metal. "Where is everyone?" she asked.

Tully slipped the harmonica into his shirt pocket. "Dirk's out catching fireflies, and your daddy went in to get us some lemonade."

"Dirk's got enough fireflies now to light the entire house. Mom and I keep letting them go again. Dirk loves this place," she added.

"And you're still not sure," Tully said, studying her face. "'Flower in the crannied wall,'" he began slowly, swinging his legs up into the pickup bed to settle himself more comfortably.

"I pluck you out of the crannies, I hold you here, root and all, in my hand Little flower..."

His hands were cupped as though he were holding the flower of which he spoke. Now he looked at her with a twinkle in his eyes.

She felt her face redden. "How did you know I looked?"

"You left the book face up. I had it face down. I'm an awful stickler for details."

"You have a terrific library," she said, masking her discomfort. Was he making fun of her?

"Glad you liked it. You're free to visit and check it out anytime. My sister is still talking about you."

"She's a precious little girl. You and Jayleen have done wonders with her."

"Not everyone agrees with you, Latina. Most of the time, she's afraid of strangers. Few people around these parts understand her the way you do, and they make thoughtless remarks. She senses the difference."

Tully was looking past her now into the darkness. Latina waited, having nothing to say and not wanting to say the wrong thing.

"Say, you left some hair-bobs on my dresser." His attention returned to her face.

"My barrettes? I'd forgotten about them."

"Althea found them. She had a fit until Mama put them in her hair. She points to them and tries to say your name."

"Really?"

"How about you and Dirk going with Althea and me on a picnic up at the millpond on Saturday? The two of you would be great for Althea. She needs to be around other people more."

Latina was on the verge of saying okay when she remembered Kent's arrival. "I have a friend coming from Mexico on his way back to the East Coast. I don't know how long he'll be staying.''

"Some other time, maybe.''

"Sure. Some other time.'' There was a pause, and Latina decided she would ask Tully what was on her mind.

"Why didn't your high school counselors help you to finish your schooling at home so you could graduate this year?'' she asked abruptly.

Tully pulled the harmonica back out of his pocket and rubbed it on his shirt sleeve. "You have to understand, Latina, that no one expects a Zell's Bush guy to graduate anyway. Most of them quit for one reason or another. I was no different.''

"But you *are*!'' she interjected with more impetus than intended. "I mean, you only quit because you *had* to.''

"They don't know the difference.''

"Did you ever consider correspondence courses? Mom and Dad could help you choose the ones you need and show you how to fill out the forms and all. Mom knows all about where to send off for them and everything.''

She stopped. He sat quietly studying the small muscial instrument in his hand. Had someone taught him to play, she wondered, or was it as natural to him as carving beauty from scraps of wood?

Presently, the clear blue eyes held hers again. "I guess you could say I threw in the towel, Latina. It seemed such a farfetched dream to think I could ever make it to college. When I saw I'd have to work full-time to pay for Althea's teacher and take care of Mama too, I closed that door in my mind completely. Not too smart, huh?''

Tully vaulted himself out of the pickup and stood to his full height. "Correspondence courses." His husky voice played over the words. "Like through the mail, right?''

She nodded.

"Latina-Flower," he said, "I believe the little door in my mind is still ajar. Let's go talk to the professors.''

It was a nerve-wracking chore to prepare a room for someone accustomed to the best, Latina thought as she gave the finishing touches to the front bedroom. She hoped Kent would appreciate the wild flowers she had carefully placed on the dresser. But then he was coming from an exclusive Acapulco hotel where they probably put long-stemmed roses in his room.

Smoothing the quilt once more, she caught sight of her nails. What a mess! There's been no reason to fix them until now. She would manicure them in time for his arrival the following afternoon. Everything would be perfect. What would her living in a farmhouse matter if she looked just right for him? Surely he liked her for who she was and not for where she lived!

A knock at the front door distracted her from her study of the room. "I'll get it," she called to her family in the kitchen. She stepped through the front room briskly, retying her wraparound skirt as she went.

She flung the heavy front door open to find Kent Starner standing there dressed in smartly creased slacks and a white blazer.

"Surprise!" he said, flashing her his wonderful smile. She wanted to slam the door. She had carefully planned to look perfect for the moment of his arrival. This couldn't be happening to her!

"Kent," she said helplessly. Her fingers touched the bandana that held back her unwashed hair. Stray wisps floated from beneath it. "I thought you said tomorrow." She forced a smile.

"Some greeting," he said. "Aren't you going to ask me in?" He bent to pick up the two pieces of matching gray-blue luggage at his feet. With his infectious grin, he said, "I'm ready for my glimpse of authentic rural Americana. Even though I got quite a dose just coming up those hills." He nodded his head toward the valley spread out below the house.

"Sure. Sure, Kent. Come on in." Awkwardly she stepped back from the door.

"A guy in our group unexpectedly decided to stay a few more days," Kent explained, setting the luggage on the braided rug in the front room. Latina watched as his eyes took everything in. "This guy was looking for someone to take his plane reservation, so I spoke up. Wanted to get here sooner to be with the most beautiful girl in the world," he added.

There it was. The charm that had won her over last summer at Periwinkle Cove. It would have been music to her ears had she felt even remotely beautiful.

Mercifully, her mother broke into the strained silence. "Who's here, Latina? Kent! Hello, there. Welcome to Zell's Bush. You're looking dashing as usual."

Catching her daughter's expression, she asked, "Weren't you due in tomorrow?"

"He caught an early flight," Latina answered for him.

"Well, no matter. We're glad to have you. Latina's been busy fixing up the front bedroom for you. It's no Waldorf Astoria, but I'm sure you'll be comfortable."

Kent laughed. "No bell hops, no room service and no choice of room. I'll try to make a go of it, Mrs. Harmen."

Just as Latina took a breath to say she'd show him the room, Tully and her dad came down the hall from the kitchen. She'd completely forgotten that Tully had been sitting at the kitchen table with her parents for the past hour sorting out which correspondence courses he should take.

Mr. Harmen made casual introductions. Latina could sense Kent's reaction to Tully. She twisted the ties of her wraparound skirt in her fingers. Tully's "Howdy" sounded so backwoodsy. Why couldn't he just say "Hi there," the way normal people did?

"I was just leaving," Tully announced, walking lightly toward the front door. "Thank you Professor and Mrs. Harmen for all your help and time. I'll head for the house now." To Kent, he added, "Hope you enjoy your stay with these fine folks."

For a breathless moment, Latina prayed Tully would exit without so much as a glance in her direction, but he paused to let his clear smiling eyes rest on her. She felt Kent looking at Tully, then at her.

"Good-bye, Latina-Flower." Those eyes were laughing at her again. Anger welled up within her. He recognized her predicament and intentionally made it worse. She stood woodenly until Tully had left, carefully closing the door behind him.

"As I was driving through all those hairpin curves," Kent commented dryly, "I felt sorry for you, being stuck out here in the sticks all alone. But I guess you weren't quite as lonely as I thought—*Latina-Flower*."

"See here, Starner," Mr. Harmen spoke up. "Tully does part-time repair work for me. He was here to see me, not Latina."

"Daddy! Really! Kent, let me show you the room we've fixed up." She gave her parents a look that let them know they could leave. Her mother ushered her father back toward the kitchen, instructing Kent to let her know if he needed anything.

Once in the front bedroom, Kent placed the smaller suitcase on the bed and opened it. From beneath the clothing, he brought out a small package and placed it in her hands. "For you," he said.

"Thank you," Latina whispered. In the box lay a pair of silver and turquoise earrings. Looking up at him, she added, "You took us by surprise, you know. But I—I'm still glad you're here."

"Sweetheart, I tried to call from the airport in Springfield, but I couldn't get through." He shrugged. "I didn't want to waste any more time, so I just came." He couldn't resist adding, "Guess I did kind of surprise you. Does King Kong spend much time around here?"

"A few evenings a week to help Dad. I never even notice when he's here." So Kent still found her attractive, in spite of old shoes, unkempt hair and nails! She gave him a teasing smile. "I guess I'll change now and get gussied up for you."

"Gussied up?" He gave a strained laugh. Not at all like the laugh she'd remembered. "Is that an Ozarkian term?" He placed his hands on her arms. "You look gussied up enough for me."

For days and weeks she'd dreamed of falling into his arms, but now she found herself pulling away. "I'll get changed and then show you around this place," she said awkwardly, avoiding his touch.

# Chapter Seven

The rental car was a new-smelling, late-model sedan with powder-blue velour upholstery. Latina slid comfortably into the luxurious interior, feeling like royalty. What would it be like to date Kent on a steady basis, she wondered. For the millionth time, she wished they lived nearer each other. Why did they have to meet on a beach hundreds of miles from their homes?

As they drove down the winding hills to the sawmill, Latina tried to explain her feelings about the millpond.

"A pond with a deserted mill," he said. "Hm. Sounds okay, I guess, if that's what turns you on. Say, sweetheart, did I tell you the color of the new sailboat? Sky blue! And it's a honey. Moves across the water like a dream. Wait'll you see what it can do." He tightened his arm around her as he maneuvered the car around the curves and bridges with one hand on the wheel. "You *are* coming out to the coast for a week or two, aren't you?" he asked.

"To the coast?" She searched her mind. Had she said something to make him think...?

"I talked to Randy last week. He said Monique's there and all the gang. It's going to be a blast. We'll arrange it with Monique's folks for you to stay there."

"I don't know, Kent. My parents—"

"They'd understand. They don't expect you to remain here in the sticks, do they?"

Latina's mother had never liked the blond, fast-talking Monique, and quite truthfully, neither had Latina. Not well enough to stay with her for a week. But even if there was someone to stay with at Periwinkle Cove, her parents would never allow her to travel alone. And on top of all that, there simply wasn't enough money for such a trip. But how could someone like Kent understand a financial crunch?

"This is the turnoff," she told him.

Kent was forced to use both hands on the wheel to negotiate the rutted drive. "Give me a six-lane expressway any day," he muttered between clenched teeth as the car lurched about.

Latina tensed at his irritation. His reference to the kids at Periwinkle Cove brought to mind the things she'd been trying to forget—that there were beautiful people out there in the summer sun while she mildewed in the soggy backwoods.

"Whew! What a layout!" he said as she led him up the path to the Garwood's front door. "This is the Zell's Bush Industrial Park, right?"

"You guessed it." She laughed, trying to join in his banter.

Etta Ann Garwood was overjoyed to see Latina and meet her "feller." Latina was relieved when Donna Dee came bouncing into the room. "Well, howdy, folks. So this is Kent. Pleased to meet you."

"Howdy," Kent retorted, obviously amused by the greeting.

"Make yourselves at home while I get some spiced cider poured up," Etta Ann said, smoothing her hands on her apron and heading for the kitchen.

Kent shook his head in disbelief, but Donna Dee was oblivious. She was chattering to Latina about the improvements in her shorthand. Some of her questions were aimed at Kent, who in return told her about his school in Vermont and his recent graduation.

"So what does a person do around here for kicks?" Kent asked during a lull in the conversation. "I mean there must be some forms of recreation somewhere."

"Oh sure!" Donna Dee nodded. "We don't just sit around picking our teeth on whittled splinters all day." Her easy joke brought a genuine laugh from Kent. "There's a nice beach and restaurant at Lake Lotawana about twenty-five miles from here."

"Lotawana? Is that name for real?"

"It's an Indian name," she explained. "The restaurant is built into the bluffs and overlooks the lake. The restaurant is done up Hawaiian-style." She made Hawaiian sound like Hi-wa-yan. Kent shot a grin at Latina that Donna Dee couldn't have missed.

"Now that sounds more our speed, doesn't it, sweetheart?" Kent said to Latina. To Donna Dee, he said, "How about if you grab a guy and come along to make it a foursome tomorrow? You show us the way. We can swim in the afternoon and eat supper there in the evening. How about it?"

Donna Dee hesitated. "Sounds swell, but I don't know."

"Hey! Starner here will foot the bill." He jabbed a thumb at his chest. "No problem. Come on. How about it? We'll be down to pick you and your date up just after lunch. You just be ready. Okay?"

Possibly only for Latina's sake, Donna Dee finally agreed.

There was no doubt in Latina's mind who Donna Dee's date would be. But there was no point telling Kent that now.

Latina awoke the next morning with a feeling of excitement. Her anxieties of the evening before had dissolved with the freshness of the morning. Today she'd be swimming with Kent just like last summer. From her dresser she pulled out her black swimsuit with the scarlet flowers.

Her mother came to her bedroom door and surveyed the unmade bed and clothes strewn about the
room.

"Oh Mom, help! What'll I wear this evening?"

She explained the day's plans and their decision to
invite Donna Dee and her date. Mrs. Harmen stepped
to the closet and pulled out her lavender shirtwaist
with the long sheer sleeves.

"This is wrinkle-resistant," she said. "Fold it into
your beach bag and you'll look great. Comb your wet
hair up on top of your head and fasten your lavender
flowers in the back."

It was a good idea, but Latina's mind was wander-
ing to Tully Clouse.

Her mother stopped talking and looked at her.
"You don't like the choice, or you're worried about
something. Which?"

"Huh? Oh, no. I mean, yes. I agree with the lavender. It'll be fine, thanks." Why did her mother have
to be so perceptive? "What's on the breakfast menu?
Kent will probably be famished."

"Ham and pancakes sound okay?"

"Mm. Great. I'll be right down to help."

When she was alone again, she clutched the lavender dress and whirled about the room on giddy feet.
How could she possibly be worried about this wonderful day? To think she would be spending it with the
most dynamic, talented, handsome guy she'd ever
known! And to think he'd come many miles out of his
way just to see her!

But when she joined her mother in the kitchen her mood had changed. Unbidden, memories of Tully came to her mind. Once again, she felt the power of his arms as he carried her through the storm, his determined blue eyes smiling encouragement at her.

"Latina, let's wait to see if everyone wants orange juice, shall we?" her mother suggested.

Without thinking, Latina had been pouring juice into the tumblers. The juice glasses hadn't even been placed around yet.

"Sorry," she muttered.

Intermittently, Latina glanced at the door, anticipating Kent's entrance. She wondered nervously what it would be like to have him at a family meal.

"You're a bit flustered, Latina. Can't you calm down?"

She gave a silly grin and laughed. "I guess not."

Her father entered with a handful of notes that he placed beside his plate. His excitement for the book was mounting daily.

"What're we waiting for?" he wanted to know.

"Well," his wife hesitated. "Dirk's not here yet."

Latina didn't know whether to wake Kent or not. He was no doubt tired after his trip.

The door to the porch slammed. "Let's eat," Dirk called. "I'm starved." He loped to the kitchen sink to wash his hands with the dishwashing detergent. Working up a lather, he blew three king-sized bubbles through his fingers before rinsing. One floated over the pancakes and burst just before touchdown, sending a fine spray over the table.

"Where's Wonderboy?" Dirk asked after he'd sat down. "Waiting for room service?" Ruthlessly he stabbed three pancakes.

"Still asleep," Latina explained coolly. "He was really tired."

"Yeah. Must be a tough drag to lounge around the beach at Acapulco. Took all his strength just to watch all those bikini beauties." Dirk helped himself generously to another pancake.

It was after eleven o'clock when Kent strolled through the house in his silk robe and matching slippers. Latina was on the back porch in a lawn chair reading.

"Hey, there you are," he called from the kitchen. He seated himself in a lawn chair beside her. "Thanks for letting me sleep. I was really tired. Say," he said, reaching to touch her hair and letting his hand rest on her shoulder. "If this is being gussied up, I'm sorry I poked fun at the term. This color is great on you."

For one frozen moment, Latina thought he was going to lean over and kiss her. His hand moved to the back of her neck and he moved his face nearer hers. "It's going to be a great day," he whispered.

With a slam of the door, Dirk exploded into the screened-in porch. "What's for lunch? I'm starved! Well, whoop-de-doo! Up in time for lunch, Mr. Starner? Great move!"

Tully's pickup was parked by the sawmill when Latina and Kent pulled into the parking lot to pick up Donna Dee.

He and Donna Dee were talking amiably as they came out of the Garwood's house, ignoring Kent who was revving the motor.

"Hill people don't move too fast, do they?" Kent said. Latina caught the mood-change in his eyes as he realized he would be spending the day with Tully Clouse.

"Pleased to see you again, Starner," Tully said, helping Donna Dee into the back seat. "Thanks for the invitation. I haven't been for a swim at Lotawana for a coon's age."

"That long, huh?" Kent said, giving him a glance. Gravel sprayed as he sped out of the lot and up the rutted drive.

Donna Dee was puzzled. "You two met already?"

"Last evening at my house," Latina explained. "Tully was talking to my dad when Kent arrived."

"Then you're already friends! That's good!"

Latina was painfully conscious of Donna Dee's pronunciation. Friends came out as "fre-yunds." She didn't dare look at Kent but she could imagine his expression all too well.

"What do you do for excitement in this thriving metropolis?" Kent asked. "Watch them stock Boles's Grocery?"

Latina tensed up, annoyed by the heavy sarcasm, but Donna Dee laughed. "It may look boring to you,

Kent," she said, "but you'd be surprised what a body can find to do when no one's around to provide the entertainment."

"I bet."

Donna Dee was right, Latina thought. Take for example her recently rediscovered joy in painting. Lack of entertainment had forced her to find her own resources.

"Sometimes," Tully's husky voice came directly behind her, "Orville and Maude get into a fight with the feather dusters. That's dandy to watch."

Donna Dee giggled. "Come on, Tully."

"Of course, Orville won't get up to defend himself. Just sits there and whacks at Maudie when she moves in too close." He gave each word an exaggerated drawl. "But she got back at him the other day! Swept him clean off his chair!"

Latina burst out laughing, but Kent only scowled. He gazed straight ahead of him, occasionally breaking his silence to swear at a particularly sharp hairpin curve or sudden bump on the road.

To Latina's surprise, Lake Lotawana was within a few minutes of Zell's Bush. They came upon it suddenly, nestled in the hills. Everyone piled out of the car to change in the little, old, rundown bathhouses. Then they all rushed to the water's edge. Kent took Latina's hand and coaxed her in. Tully and Donna Dee had already dived in ahead of them and were swimming toward the center of the lake.

The feel of Kent's hand, the look on his face, even the teasing tone of his voice, brought back to Latina her precious memories of the summer before. For a long time they floated together in the water, too relaxed and lazy even to talk. Finally, by unspoken mutual consent, they swam to the shore and walked hand in hand to the warm rocks where they had left their towels.

"You know the millpond I told you about last evening?" Latina asked, shaking a miniature waterfall from her hair.

"The one with the deserted mill?" Kent asked, carefully spreading his towel and lowering himself down on it.

"Yes. Would you believe I've been painting it? It's quite a challenge. There's a mist over the water and a cavelike overhang. The light is pretty tricky—"

"That's a real shame, sweetheart." Lying on his stomach now, Kent's voice was muffled into his arm.

"It's a what?" Had she heard him wrong?

He rolled over and looked at her. "Man, it's a shame there's nothing more for you to do than go off alone and paint. You'll get paranoid that way. Are you sure your folks won't let you stay with Monique for a week? They can't expect you to rot in this forsaken place just because your dad's a history nut."

Latina's shoulders stiffened. She had been furious with her father for ruining her summer, but she admired his work intensely.

"I don't know, Kent. I really doubt if they'll let me go."

He groaned and turned over again and gazed out at the water. "This is nothing like Periwinkle Cove, huh?"

She wanted to agree, but she also wanted to tell him that she thought the lake was beautiful. Couldn't there be room for both? Did one have to be better than the other? "But you'll soon be back where the waves are pounding, Kent," she said.

Far to her left, where the rocks and bluffs jutted out from a steep cliffwall beneath the restaurant, she saw Tully's form on the rocks. He executed a perfect dive into the water.

"That's not for a week yet," Kent said, moving into a sitting position. He looked at her, then out to the rocks, then back at her. "You aren't trying to get rid of me, are you?" he asked accusingly.

She laid her head against his warm shoulder. "Never."

A fat candle anchored in a pink seashell flickered on their small table, part of the Polynesian décor of the Kona Kai restaurant. Latina couldn't think of any place in Periwinkle Cove that was as elegant. She stirred her juice cooler and wondered if Tully and Donna Dee were ill at ease. She hoped they would not do or say anything that would cause Kent to make fun of them.

Tully ordered fried chicken for Donna Dee and himself. Latina could see the disdain in Kent's face as he ordered an exotic sounding fish dish for himself. His silence as they ate bordered on a sullenness that Latina wanted to shake out of him.

After eating, Kent took her to dance on the terrace overlooking the lake. "Bruisers like Clouse are usually afraid of their own shadows," he told her. "The bigger they are, the harder they fall, you know."

Oh Kent! she thought. Don't make matters worse. But she realized Kent was seeing Tully as she had that first week. How could he know Tully would brave a raging storm to rescue a rain-soaked stranger, or that he would give up his high-school graduation for the sake of his little sister? "Sometimes that holds true and sometimes it doesn't," she said.

"For Clouse, it is undoubtedly the former."

Latina stepped back from his grasp. "It may interest you to know, Kent, that I couldn't care less if Tully Clouse is afraid of his shadow or not." Abruptly, she spun on her heel and strode to the railing at the edge of the dance floor.

Kent came briskly in pursuit. "Hey, Latina." His voice had softened. "Look, I'm sorry." Gently he took hold of her arms and turned her around to face him. "You can't blame a fellow for being jealous, can you? Here you are stuck out in the hills with a guy like that. He's not just your regular Joe. If you know what I mean."

"I suppose I should be flattered," she said, but she felt more threatened than flattered.

"So what's on the agenda for tomorrow, sweetheart," he said, guiding her by the elbow to a terrace table.

Latina took a breath. "How about a picnic by the millpond?"

"Somehow that doesn't sound too swinging. Tramping through mosquito-infested jungles just see a run-down mill. I'd sort of thought we could drive up to Springfield for the day."

Latina's heart plummeted. Her parents would never agree to her going that far alone with a boy—any boy. The dancers on the terrace were swaying to a melancholy tune that seeped into her consciousness and made her want to cry.

"We could shop in the afternoon and stay for a concert in the evening. Something's certain to be popping up there. What say?"

"It's out of the question, Kent. My parents would never let me go that far from home on a date." She dared not look at his face. Instead, she stared out at the black velvety water. What must he think of her? "Our friends will think we've left them behind," she said in an unsteady voice. She pushed away from the table and stood up.

"Not a bad idea," Kent said harshly. He followed her back to the dinng room.

Donna Dee brightened when she saw them returning. "Welcome back. We thought you'd jumped overboard."

Latina prayed her cheeks were not as flushed as they felt, for Tully's searching eyes were looking clear through her.

"Guess we'll call it a night, gang," Kent announced, making no move to reseat himself at the table. He picked up the check from beside his plate. "Separate checks? Where's the other one, Clouse? I'll catch it. This one's on me."

Tully patted his shirt pocket. "Appreciate the offer, but I can handle it."

Latina hated to think of his spending that precious money he'd worked so hard to earn. Jayleen and Althea needed so many things—he couldn't afford to spend it on a senseless outing. This wild comedy of errors was making her more miserable by the minute.

"But Clouse," Kent was protesting. "I didn't want...I didn't think...." The more he struggled to speak, the more obvious it became that he assumed Tully had no money.

Tully's laughing eyes creased at the corners. He rose to his full height, leaned toward Kent and said in a husky whisper, "It's stash money what them revenooers ain't tuk from me yet. You don't go squealing on me now, y'hear?"

Donna Dee laughed. "Oh Tully, you sound exactly like Grandpa Gar."

"The guy's a real scream," Kent said in Latina's ear, pushing her firmly toward the cash register.

The drive back to Zell's Bush was relatively quiet, except for Tully and Donna Dee making soft conversation in the back seat. After letting Donna Dee out at the saw mill, Latina and Kent were followed by Tully's noisy pickup as they drove over the inclines and around the bridges to the Nettleton farm, where Tully lumbered past them and gave a farewell *beep beep*.

Latina wondered if Kent would want to take a walk in the moonlight. If only she could do something to ease the strain between them!

But without a word, he helped her out and led her in the front door where her parents were waiting up, playing some silly board game. If only they had gone to bed! Then she could have talked to him immediately. Kent excused himself and retired to his room.

Certain that her parents sensed the tension between them, Latina wanted to escape before they could ask embarrassing questions.

"Have a good time?" her mother asked.

"Great," Latina answered, heading up the stairway and closing the door to her room. Tomorrow, she would ask her father about letting her go to Springfield. He might say yes. On the other hand, after resting and thinking about it, Kent might want to go see the millpond. Once he saw the sun sparkling on the water and the rainbows dancing in the hanging mist, he'd love it as much as she did.

The next morning she was wakened by Kent's muffled voice on the phone at the foot of the stairs. She dressed quickly and ran downstairs, where she found Kent about to step out from the front bedroom. His luggage was sitting by the door.

"Oh, Latina. There you are." His tone was distant. "I'm sorry. I was just calling my folks, and guess what's happened?"

"I couldn't. Suppose you tell me."

"My dad wants me to get out to the coast right away. Something's come up and he needs me. I'll have to leave right after breakfast."

# Chapter Eight

Kent's eyes avoided hers as he loaded his luggage and climbed into the now-dusty rental car. She was glad he didn't say something dumb like, "It's been great seeing you," or "Hope we can do it again sometime," or even, "I'll be seeing you." He simply said "I'm sorry, Latina. Good-bye."

She watched the dust rise as the car made its way down the rocky drive before going back to the house to throw out the wild flowers and strip the bed. From now until September, it would be a matter of survival. The one dream she'd counted on to sustain her for the summer had gone up in smoke. She never expected to hear from Kent again.

Strangely enough, she sought refuge in the bosom of the hills. Almost daily, she packed a sandwich and a thermos, and carried her art paraphernalia to the solitude of the millpond. She couldn't bear to be around her family. They were probably thinking it was best that Kent left. After all, they hadn't liked him in the first place.

Over and over again, she rehearsed the two days of Kent's stay, attempting to figure out what had gone wrong. If only she had welcomed him with open arms the moment he appeared at the door. Then he might never have given Tully a second thought. But the damage was done. She would never forgive herself for the mess she'd made.

Her painting no longer engaged her. Often, she simply sat on the rock overhang, staring and thinking.

A noisy mockingbird had been a frequent visitor to Latina's retreat, many times daring to come down on the lowest boughs of the willows. One afternoon when she was hard at work, he chanced to come down beside her. She put aside her brushes and tossed him bits of bread from her lunch. Before he had devoured it, Latina grabbed the sketchbook and quickly drew his charcoal body, studying closely the stark black trim on his wings and tail. The bird came to life through the pen in her fingers.

He continued to share her lunch and was later joined by a squirrel looking for a handout. Could they sense, as had Althea, that she was no threat? The animals trusted Tully. It seemed they trusted her too.

Tully had received his first lessons back in the mail and was on his way to receiving his diploma. Latina, however, avoided talking to him, paying little attention to his comings and goings. Her mother had stepped into the role of personal tutor and chief support.

Donna Dee was Latina's only real friend. The girls enjoyed long walks together, as well as more domestic activities, such as shelling peas, husking sweet corn and breaking up "snap" beans—which Latina learned were plain old green beans.

One evening, they were sitting on the Garwood's front porch watching the sun set. Latina had been talking of her painting when Donna Dee said, "I've told Daddy about your work, and he says he'll pay you to do a picture of the sawmill and the house and all. What do you think?"

When Latina didn't answer, she added, "It may not look like much to some people," she made a sweeping wave with her arm, "but he's proud of every inch.

Latina considered it. Could she really paint something that would please Mr. Garwood? Finally, she answered. "Actually," she said, "I'm not that good. I'm just a novice."

"How about if you let Daddy judge? Do up some little sketches for him, then he can say yes or no."

So it was by invitation that Latina found herself the next week on the hill opposite the sawmill rather than at her millpond. In the clearing where she sat, she had a bird's-eye view of the valley. She surveyed the mill thoughtfully and wondered if it was possible to capture something for which she had no appreciation or real interest.

Under the vast open sheds, the saws screamed. The Garwood's small house sat rakishly on the hillside above them, connected only by the worn path that wound down the hill. On the far side of the house lay Etta Ann's garden, mushrooming in the summer sun. Out near the sawdust piles was the brick tool shed with its peaked roof. Everything was disjointed and scattered. She sighed. She'd best go down and tell Mr. Garwood right now she could never do this.

A low rumble announced the arrival from out of the hills of a semitrailer loaded with logs. The mill came to life as Mr. Garwood shouted instructions to the men for unloading. The movements prompted Latina's hands and mind as she sketched the activity around the truck. By noon, three false starts were lying in wadded clusters around her and the fourth attempt was beginning to come together.

At the sound of the noon whistle, the workers congregated under the shade trees near the sawdust piles to each lunch. Latina rummaged in her case for her own lunch that she'd brought along.

Presently, she noticed Tully walking to his pickup and getting his books and papers, evidently planning to study as he ate. He settled against a tree trunk.

"Just take a gander at Clouse there, fellas," she heard Collier say tauntingly. The words were distinct in the warm summer air, in spite of the distance from her spot on the hillside down to the mill. "Thinks he's better than us 'cause he reads some old words on paper. Ain't that the foolest notion you ever heard of?"

From what Latina could make out, the other men were ignoring Collier's outburst. But the dark-haired boy wasn't satisfied. Jumping to his feet, he grabbed papers from Tully's lap. "Let's see here what you got, Professor Clouse. You been hanging around them city folks at Nettleton's so much, you're beginning to think like them."

Tully reached out to grab the papers, but not quickly enough. He said something that was inaudible to Latina.

Collier's high-pitched voice, however, was quite clear. "Don't get in a tizzy now, cousin. I just want to check this stuff out, to see you're doing it proper."

Latina's fists clenched as she watched the drama. How she longed to see Tully flatten his cousin and shut him up!

"You can't read them papers, anyhow, Hunsecker," one of the workers hooted.

"I could so!" he countered sharply. "But who wants to? It's just a bunch of dumb trash!" Then like a vengeful child, Collier began ripping pages and tossing them into the wind.

Silently, Tully rose, walked to the dusty blue pickup, got inside, and sat there reading a textbook.

"Don't worry, Clouse," Collier shouted after him. "It don't take no smarts to raise up a dim-witted sister!"

Latina was incensed. How could Tully let Collier get away with it? Had Kent been right about Tully being afraid of his own shadow? It seemed he couldn't even stand up to his cousin! Well, there was nothing much she could do about it. She gathered up her materials and started home.

That evening, she bent over the sketches at her desk. She fleshed out the faint marks she'd made of the sawmill that afternoon. No breeze came in from her bedroom windows, and her blouse clung to her back. She massaged her tired neck and shoulders with her fingertips. It was time for a break.

Slipping into the kitchen, she poured herself a glass of lemonade. From the porch, she could hear her mother talking to Tully, who was wresting one of the screens from its place. "Will you be ready to mail that composition by tomorrow, Tully?" Mrs. Harmen asked.

His answer was slow in coming. "Looks like it'll take a few more days, ma'am," he said.

"But I thought you were nearly finished."

"Something came up," Tully called back over his shoulder as he carried the screen out to the sawhorse where her father was attaching new wire.

Something came up all right, Latina agreed silently. A loathsome cousin named Collier came up. Came right up and destroyed the composition in two seconds flat.

Latina's bare feet stepped quietly on the linoleum floor, as she replaced the pitcher in the refrigerator. She heard Tully laugh. "Now don't you give me no gosh-awful dunce cap, mizz schoolmarm," he said.

It was the same act he'd pulled with Kent, only Kent hadn't thought it very funny.

From out in the yard, her father said, "Don't forget, Paulie, this boy has to do more than just study."

"Of course, you're right," she agreed. "I guess I'm getting too anxious. I won't pressure you, Tully. You're doing a great job."

"Say, Latina!" Tully startled her. She'd thought she couldn't be seen, but he must have seen her step across the doorway. They had hardly spoken since the day at the lake.

"Hello," she said. "Working hard?"

"You daddy sees to that. He's a slave driver."

"You don't seem to be suffering much."

"The only suffering he's experiencing is acute thirst," her mother said. "I'll get the lemonade."

While she stepped inside, Tully thrust his torso through the window where the screen had been. "Althea and I want to know if you and Dirk are ready to go on that picnic with us?"

"When?"

"This Saturday."

"I don't think we had anything planned," she said carefully.

"Saturday, it is then."

Latina prayed her brother would make no wisecracks about Kent in front of Tully. She had planned to warn him against it, but at that moment the blue pickup rumbled up the drive and she changed her mind. It would be just like Dirk to do it to irk her.

Tully hopped out to greet them with his customary "Howdy."

Dirk opted to ride in the back, and Althea crawled into Latina's arms, her head bobbing and her eyes bright with excitement. In her baby-fine hair were the two barrettes.

Tully parked just off the bridge where Latina first discovered the path to the water's edge. Jayleen had packed lunch in an oversized, antiquated basket, which Dirk offered to carry.

The four of them followed the stream's pebbled path until the water widened out and forced them to the underbrush. She and Tully took turns carrying Althea, as Tully informed Dirk which of the trees were water tupelos and which were river birches. He pointed out the dogwood and the red oak, and the delicate ferns along the bank.

Latina let Althea walk a ways through a clearing, holding tightly to her hand.

"Fwy! Fwy!" she squealed.

"A butterfly. Yes, Althea," Latina answered.

Her attention diverted, Latina missed seeing Tully lunge toward Dirk, but she heard Dirk give a heavy "oof!" as the two of them hit the ground.

"What on earth... Dirk, are you all right?"

"I think so." He slowly sat up. "And I think I see..." He was pointing a few feet from where his next steps would have taken him. There lay a wicked, yawning steel trap.

Latina gasped.

"Sorry fella," Tully said, ruffling Dirk's hair. "But I had to get you stopped."

Grabbing a nearby stick, he triggered the mechanism. The resounding crack set a shudder through Latina. She hugged Althea.

"Collier's work?" she asked, venturing nearer.

"Yep," Tully answered, his eyes meeting hers.

"Who's Collier?" Dirk demanded. "Must not be too smart if he leaves things like this lying around." He dangled the trap at the end of its chain, making a harsh rattling sound.

"Collier Hunsecker is my cousin, Dirk."

"Oh, sorry."

"That's okay. You're right. This isn't the time nor the place to set traps."

Tully lifted Althea to his shoulders, allowing her laughter to mask the tension. But in her mind, Latina still envisioned the wicked trap and the sharp teeth. Supposing it had been little, helpless Althea!

"Wow, sis!" Dirk gave a low whistle as they stepped from the curtain of trees to the millpond. "This is neat!"

Although he was obviously itching to cross over and explore the mill, he offered to watch Althea while lunch was being spread out on the large flat rocks beneath the overhang. His newfound manners surprised Latina.

Jayleen's touch was evident in the lunch of fried chicken, deviled eggs and fresh fruit pies. At the bottom of the basket was a note—"Latina, I love you. Thanks. Jayleen."

Latina glanced to see if Tully noticed her reading it, but he was rolling a large log up onto the rocks. "For my backrest," he said.

Lunch filled even the bottomless Dirk. The mockingbird flew noisily down for his share. Althea's face was decorated with blackberry filling from her pie, which she ate with great skill. Latina observed how Tully helped her, but never prevented her from helping herself.

Later, Dirk received permission to explore the mill, and Althea curled up against Tully's chest and fell asleep.

As Latina gathered the lunch scraps and repacked the basket, she remembered the note and handed it to Tully to see. His blue eyes lit up. "She means that, Latina. Says she never saw Althea take to anyone like she has to you."

"I love Althea, and she knows it. But Tully, I really think we should think of her safety—that trap—"

"I was keeping a close watch. I don't miss much."

"Sometimes other people are coming through here when you aren't keeping watch," she retorted.

"I'm on Collier's heels most of the time, Latina. Releasing what he's set."

"You weren't on his heels on that one," she said. "Tully, it's wrong. How can you let him get away with it?"

"Collier's got a hurting way down deep inside that makes him mean. Not much you can do about a thing like that."

"That hurting—did it make him tear up your composition?" She stepped to the edge of the rocks, pulled off her tennis shoes and dangled her feet in the cold water.

"You don't miss much, either."

She looked back at him. He was still smiling. "I just happened to be on the hill across the road, doing sketches for Mr. Garwood. I saw the whole thing. If you let him get away with things like that, it'll make him worse. You can't tolerate wrong and hope it will go away. What makes him so hateful anyway?"

"His daddy did it to him a long time ago."

"Where's his father now?"

"Long gone. Ran out on him and his mama and brothers. Just ran out. But not before he did a heap of damage to Collier."

"How?"

Althea awakened and came to Latina, winding her thin arms about her neck and snuggling up close. Tully then moved to sit beside Latina on the rocks. "Collier's daddy, Rendy Hunsecker, was sweet on his own wife's sister. He was a sorry husband and father."

"His wife's sister?"

"My mama. Jayleen."

"Did she love him?"

"Nope. She had eyes only for Aaron Clouse." His husky voice grew reverent. "The world's greatest."

After a moment, he went on. "Collier's daddy always put me up to him without mercy—always telling Collier he didn't do things as good as I did, and asking why he couldn't be more like me. My daddy told him it was wrong, but Uncle Rendy wouldn't listen. Stubborn. Loved Mama so much he was blind—and deaf to hearing truth.

"When my daddy passed on, Uncle Rendy was there on our porch the day after the funeral telling us he was going to get a divorce and wanted to marry Mama right away." Tully gave a little snort. "When Mama pointed him to the road and told him not to come back, he sort of went crazy. Beat Collier up pretty bad, then disappeared. He's never been back."

Tully paused and reached over to stroke Althea's hair. "So you see, Latina, Collier can't look at me in a right light. He never will be able to because of his daddy making me his enemy all these years."

"Still, it's not fair," Latina said hotly. "Collier needs to be turned in and prosecuted for breaking the law."

"Could be," Tully answered. "But I figure if you give a man enough rope, he'll hang himself. Collier's trapping brings him money of his own. He feels it's his right since he's had such a rough time of things. I don't bother him much. Just take wounded animals that aren't dead and release traps that are near the pathways."

Excited calls from Dirk interrupted the conversation. It was coming from behind them. "Tully! Latina! Come here and hurry!"

Tully swept Althea up in his arms and Latina followed. Dirk was kneeling over a young raccoon whose leg was in the teeth of a steel trap.

"Can you get him out?" Dirk asked.

"Sure can. Move back a bit. Latina, take Althea."

It took several tries before Tully pressed open the trap. Within moments, the furry creature was safe in Dirk's arms. Before Latina could protest, Tully tore his shirt to wrap a bandage around the injured leg.

"Can I keep him?" Dirk asked.

"I don't see why not. I'll give you one of my cages. When his leg heals, you'll have a sweet pet. He's still young enough that you can tame him." Tully rubbed the raccoon's furry ear.

"Neat! Thanks, Tully!"

Latina moved nearer so Althea could touch the animal. As she touched him, she felt the trembling of his little body. How cruel to harm such a helpless creature!

Later in the afternoon, when the four of them emerged from the cool of the woods to the dusty road, a rusty pickup came rumbling around the curve, rolling up a cloud of dust behind it. When the driver spied the small party beside the road, the vehicle came to a stop and Collier jumped out onto the bridge.

"Howdy, Tully," he said. "Where you been?" He spoke to Tully, but his dark eyes were on Dirk and the furry bundle in his arms.

"We took Althea on a picnic," Tully answered.

"Well, now. I see you been messing with my traps. You ought not done that. You're gonna get yourself in all sorts of trouble." Standing before Dirk, he glared at him. "Hand over my coon!"

"He's mine! I found him," Dirk said.

Collier moved closer to Dirk. "Any traps in that valley are mine. You ought not mess with my animals or my traps, kid. Now give him over."

With an easy grace, Tully stepped beside Dirk. "Leave him alone, Collier! If it's coons you're wanting, you know I got a barn full of them."

"You're so uppity, Tully Clouse! Act like you're special just because you can read and study some!" He paused for a moment before turning toward his truck. "I'll get you for this, wait and see," he muttered. The tires of his truck spun in the gravel as he gunned his truck over the rattling bridge.

# Chapter Nine

Latina stood at her window watching her father lay the wood for their Fourth of July bonfire. Her family had been pleased with her suggestion to invite the Garwoods and the Clouses over for the evening.

No doubt they would have just planned another fishing excursion. How unimaginative! She felt a little smug as she observed the backyard preparations in progress. Tables had been constructed out of planks resting across sawhorses, and Etta Ann had brought over brightly colored tablecloths to cover them.

Perhaps this would be the night that Tully would really notice her, Latina thought as she brushed her hair until it fell softly around her shoulders. She wished they could begin again in their relationship, that he would put behind him the awful weekend with Kent.

Slipping her feet into her white flats, she hurried downstairs.

The Garwoods arrived first. She could hear the friendly conversation in the backyard as she stood at the sink cutting carrot sticks. Donna Dee was helping put food out on the tables.

"Howdy, Latina. You sure look nice," Tully said, walking into the kitchen with a big wicker picnic basket.

"Thanks, Tully. All the food goes out back." She nodded toward the back door, trying to think of something to say to keep him there talking to her, but her mind went blank.

He moved on through to the back door, snitching a carrot stick on the way and giving her a broad smile.

When she carried out the relish plate later, Tully was checking on Dirk's pet coon, while Mr. Garwood looked on.

As soon as she had helped serve, Latina took Althea to a lawn chair and helped her eat. As she wiped catsup from the little girl's face, she wondered what would become of Jayleen and Althea after Tully left for college. Already, her mother had mentioned that Tully could apply for scholarships at Eagleton College. How would Jayleen and her handicapped child fare for themselves? Perhaps it had been a mistake for her parents to interfere in this way. Her father had said that if Tully were able to find a job in Eagleton and had scholarship money, he could perhaps send money home to help Jayleen. Latina wasn't sure that would be enough. Tully did the bulk of the shopping for Jayleen, plus many other chores around the house.

Later, the bonfire had burned down to a reddish-blue heap of glowing embers, and the guests sat around it, lethargic from the effect of so much food. Dirk had a bulging pocket of firecrackers, but when asked about them, he explained he'd decided to wait until the next day to shoot them because "they might disturb Coony and Althea."

Latina studied her long-legged brother, who must have grown a full two inches since their arrival, and wondered if this was the same boy who used to insist on getting his own way. Her entire family was changing, she thought, as she saw her father move his lawn chair closer to his wife and put an arm around her shoulder. Was it the effect of the quiet beauty of the hills? Or the selfless fortitude of the people they had come to know? Perhaps both. She looked at Tully's strong face reflected by the glow of the fire.

He must have felt her gaze, for he looked back and smiled. She wanted so much to know what he thought of her, and yet she was afraid to ask.

Tully helped her father and Mr. Garwood with the fireworks display in the front yard. Shortly after the spectacle was over and they had returned to the back-yard, Latina saw Tully walking with Donna Dee down the long driveway, their outlines barely visible in the moonlight. She supressed her jealousy by reminding herself how much she loved Donna Dee.

Althea was asleep in Jayleen's arms when the party began to break up. Latina helped carry the picnic basket to the pickup for her. Repeatedly, Jayleen thanked Latina for the evening. "I can't remember when I've had such a nice time. Before we lost Aaron, I suppose. You've been such a blessing, Latina."

"I'm glad you enjoyed yourself. It was fun having you," Latina told her, embarrassed by the praise.

"I wouldn't have missed it for the world," she said, settling herself and the sleeping Althea into the pickup.

"Me neither," Tully said as he strode toward them and hopped in beside his mother.

"Oh, Latina, I just remembered," Jayleen said. "Miss Wilkes, Althea's teacher, wants to meet you. I told her about how you made up to Althea so quick and she said she wanted to get to know you."

"Fine. Anytime. I'll be there." She was hoping Tully would say something about another picnic, but instead, he was saying they'd better get Althea home since she was "plumb tuckered out."

For a time after the guests had left, Latina sat alone in the yard, poking at the dying embers with one of the wiener-roasting sticks and staring at the spray of sparks she created. Now that the evening had come and gone, it seemed rather anticlimactic. The entire thing had been her idea, and she knew everyone had had fun, but it had disturbed her to see Tully and Donna Dee together. If they were serious about each other, was Donna Dee planning to wait for Tully until he finished college?

Her thoughts returned to Kent. Now he seemed more a memory than a person. She realized she'd never known him at all. They had never talked of things that mattered, but always of shallow things of no consequence.

She thought again of Tully. At what precise moment had her feelings toward him changed? Was it when she saw his room filled with books and wood carvings? Or the moment he saved Dirk from the trap. Perhaps it had been...

She was startled by a sharp snap in the dense darkness behind her. Dropping the stick into the fire, she ran into the house and up to her room. Would she ever feel completely safe in the swallowing-up hills?

The next morning she wakened to her brother's anguished cries. She jumped out of bed, snatched her robe, and ran down the stairs out the back door and onto the wet grass. She pushed past her parents to see his precious Coony lying on the grass. She turned away the moment she saw the bloodied fur.

Her father took a closer look. "Someone pried open the clasp and then stabbed the little thing," he said.

Mrs. Harmen held Dirk and consoled him. "Who would do such a terrible thing?" she demanded.

"His name is Collier Hunsecker," Latina said. "He's Tully's cousin. The same guy who set the trap that caught Coony in the first place." She thought of the noise behind her the night before and shivered. Had Collier been watching them all evening?

In fragmented sentences, Dirk told how Collier had demanded the animal be given back to him. "I should have kept Coony on the back porch during the night," he said, catching his breath. "Then he would have been safe."

"Even if you had," Latina put in, "he would have found another way to get even. Collier's got a mad on all the time," she explained, using Donna Dee's expression.

"Let's hope he's had his revenge now and leaves us alone," Mrs. Harmen said.

Dirk slammed a clenched fist into his palm. "I'm going to help Tully release all of Collier's traps from now on! That guy needs to be stopped."

When Tully learned of the incident a few days later, he apologized for Collier. "Don't hold him responsible," he told the Harmen family. "He's bitter because he didn't get his own way. If you're willing to let Dirk have another pet, he can have the pick of what I have up at the barn. Collier never touches the ones I have. He knows better."

Although Tully's offer appeased Dirk and her parents, Latina couldn't forget Collier's act of cruelty. She thought of calling the Wildlife Officials and turning him in. But if he found out who had testified against him, what other dreadful thing would he do?

Shortly after the Fourth of July picnic, on a Saturday morning, Latina was in the Garwood's living room with the proposed sketches spread out on the claw-footed dining table.

Etta Ann flitted about, getting them glasses of cold cider and peering over her husband's shoulder at the sketches and muttering, "My, my, would you look at that."

Latina had hoped Donna Dee would be there to act as a liaison; but Etta Ann explained that she had gone to the Clouse's for a visit.

When the decisions were made on which pictures she should pursue, Latina left quickly. As she was leaving, Donna Dee drove up. "Latina!" her friend called out. "Did he like them?"

"Sort of, I guess. At least he wants me to go ahead on a couple."

"Let me see," she said eagerly, taking the sketches from Latina's hand. "These are good, Latina. If you only knew how hard it is to please Daddy, you'd know it's more than 'sort of' with him."

"You really think so?"

"And you're a hit with Althea, too. All she can talk about is 'Ah-teen-a.'"

Latina smiled. "The feeling's mutual."

"It's great for Jayleen, too. Not many people around here accept Althea like you have. It's not their fault, of course. They have old-fashioned ideas that if someone has children that can't act right, they ought to hide them away."

"That's hard on Jayleen, isn't it?"

Donna Dee nodded her curly head. "Very hard."

"I've thought about helping her," Latina confided, "but I didn't want to barge in."

"She's up there alone with Althea every day, Latina. You can be sure you'd be welcome anytime you went to visit. I used to go up there more often before I started working." After a moment, she added, "Have you heard that Miss Wilkes wants to meet you?"

"I heard. Jayleen told me the other evening. At first, I was doubtful. But now I'm anxious to meet her too. I've wondered what type of person travels into these hills to teach a handicapped child."

"You'll like her," Donna Dee said. "She's a sweet person just like you." The two shared an affectionate hug before Latina left, and again she thought of how her friendship with this backwoods girl had literally saved her summer.

Later that day, seated out by the road in front of the farmhouse, she flipped through her most recent sketchbook. She was confident that her style was improving, but she needed guidance. It had never occurred to her to study art, but now it didn't seem like such a bad idea. Possibly she could fit it in into her fall schedule. She'd talk to her mother about it very soon.

One sketch in her book was of Tully and Dirk preparing the cage for Coony. She'd been out in the yard in one of the green lawn chairs watching them work. At first, she attempted to draw the raccoon's masked face, which she did quite successfully. But then she found herself sketching out Tully's square jaw and his thick sandy hair. The mouth was not too great a challenge, nor was his straight nose, but his eyes—what pencil or brush could ever capture the understanding in those clear, blue eyes?

She was sketching the farmhouse when a strange car pulled in. The light film of dust proclaimed that it wasn't a local. The driver, a young lady, waved at her. As Latina left her place in the grass and walked to the car, the lady called, "Are you Latina Harmen?"

"Yes, I am," she answered, closing her sketchbook.

"I'm Beverly Wilkes, Althea's tutor."

She was much younger than Latina had imagined. They shook hands through the car window.

"I'd like to visit with you if you have a minute."

"Sure," Latina agreed. "Let's go up to the house."

Miss Wilkes opened the door to offer her a ride up the long drive. Getting in, Latina surveyed the stranger with interest. Her light-blond hair was brushed back from her face in a casual style and she was dressed in a lightweight suit and low-heeled pumps. Her efficient manner and appearance gained Latina's immediate approval.

After introductions were made with her parents, Mr. Harmen retreated to his study and Miss Wilkes sat visiting with Latina and her mother. She came right to the point. "From what Jayleen tells me, you have an affinity with Althea, Latina; it seems you possess a natural talent for working with handicapped children."

"I've not been around them all that much. All I know is that Althea is easy to love and that the Clouses do a great job of teaching her."

"You're very perceptive, Latina. However, even with the insight they possess, they're still isolated with the child. Most of the townspeople are not sympathetic toward them and Jayleen gets lonely." Her comments confirmed what Donna Dee had said earlier. "It occurred to me that Jayleen might attempt to take Althea on a shopping trip if you were there to help. Or perhaps even out to lunch in Palatka."

"I'd like to, Miss Wilkes. I've been wanting to help them more."

"Please, call me Beverly. I had an idea you'd agree." The joy in this teacher's face indicated more than just a casual interest in a student. "You're an unselfish girl, Latina, and your life will be enriched for having helped them. But I'm sure you already know that."

"I'm just not sure, Latina. Being with Althea here at home or out in the woods is different from taking her into a crowd. People stare. It's hard."

"Come on, I'll help you. You can shop and I'll stay with her in the car, then we'll meet Donna Dee for lunch. We'd only spend a few hours."

At the sound of her name, Althea laughed and muttered to herself.

"Someday, Althea will be out in the world more than ever. Wouldn't now be the best time to prepare her?" Latina asked gently.

"You're right, of course. And I'm grateful for your offer."

Within the hour the three set off. Latina was thankful the car was air-conditioned for the day hot and muggy. Althea's balance was such that Jayleen had to carry her on her lap the entire way to Palatka. Latina knew that task in itself was enough to tire a person. Althea bounced and wiggled and jabbered, sensing something special was in store.

Jayleen made several purchases, giving Latina directions to the various stores. At first, Latina stayed in the car with Althea, but later with Jayleen's permission, she took her into the grocery store. Latina marveled at her alertness and eagerness to learn. Although her speech was badly slurred, Latina was interpreting her meanings more clearly than ever.

At the last stop before they met Donna Dee for lunch, Althea accidentally bumped the car's horn as they waited outside. Latina chuckled at the surprise registered on Althea's face. The little girl studied the steering wheel intently to see where the noise had come from. Her clumsy hands groped for the steering column.

Carefully, Latina took hold of her hand and made it press again on the horn. The child's face lit up with excitement. She knew she had done it. She had made the noise work. Suddenly, it became a game that Latina didn't know if she could stop.

Presently, Jayleen returned to the car and took her daughter onto her lap. "Getting impatient?" she asked.

"That was your daughter honking." Latina explained how easily Althea had followed the instructions. They were still laughing over the incident when they entered the cool recesses of the walnut-paneled restaurant.

Donna Dee had reserved a table. After they had ordered sandwiches and salads, they enjoyed some casual women's talk. Althea sat between them in a toddler's seat with her thin legs hanging past the footrest. She smiled and babbled happily, relishing every bite she was fed.

After their pleasant lunch, Donna Dee hurried back to her office and Latina and Jayleen loaded Althea into the car to return to the hills. It had been a good day and a landmark for Jayleen.

"I'd never have mustered up the courage to go without your help," she told Latina as she lifted Althea out of the car at the Clouse home. "I don't know how I can ever thank you. You came along at just the right time in our lives. To think we have Miss Wilkes helping us, and now you. I keep pinching myself to see if I'm dreaming."

Latina declined Jayleen's offer to come in for a time. She helped carry the parcels inside, then hurried home.

She found her father in the front room with a lap full of file folders. He greeted her with a big smile. "Hi, Latina. Have a good day in the city?"

"I had a *great* day in the city, Dad. That is, if you call Palatka a city!" Flopping into the nearest chair, she described the day.

Her father leaned back, listening intently. "I'm really impressed by what you're doing for Jayleen and her daughter, Latina," he said.

"Thanks, Dad." She stood up to go. "I'd better get changed before I melt."

"By the way," her father said, "I've been smelling paint fumes coming from the room next to mine. You've been pretty secretive about what's going on in there. I think Parke Garwood's seen more of your work than I have."

"You've been a little secretive too," she retorted, referring to the stacks of files and papers strewn about.

He lifted a bulging file from his lap. "There are some fascinating things in here. Would it interest you to know that it was Tully's great-grandfather who built the old mill with its elegant waterwheel?"

Latina lowered herself back into the chair. "I'd be *very* interested," she replied. "And what about the Nettletons? Have you dug up anything about them?"

"As a matter of fact, I have. But I asked first." He stood and reached out a hand to her. "Let's go see your paintings."

Having her father review her work was more unsettling than presenting them to Mr. Garwood. After all, Mr. Garwood simply wanted to see his sawmill on canvas.

"Mm," her father mumbled around his pipe stem. "Mm, hm." He lingered over the sketches and paintings. There were several of the millpond, two of the sawmill and various ones of the house and other scenes that had caught her fancy. The one of Tully was purposely left under the bed. That was hers alone.

"Latina, these are good."

She let her breath out slowly.

"In fact, they're very good." Her father held his pipe and looked at her. "So good that I'd like to ask your permission to submit a few of them along with my manuscript to use as possible illustrations for the book."

"I'd be honored to be associated with such a fine historian, Professor Harmen. Thanks, Dad." She threw her arms about him.

"Now," he said, clearing his throat, "come and see what I've uncovered. Some of these things will astonish you."

That evening, Latina read file after file of notes her father had collected about Zell's Bush and its people.

As she read, she marveled at the courage and the stamina of the ones who'd settled in this rugged land. And knowing some of their descendants personally, she could see how the courage still flowed in their veins.

She had come to a new appreciation of her father's work—and now she had an opportunity to have a small part in it.

# Chapter Ten

The cool of the millpond was delightfully refreshing. The intense July heat had not even penetrated the protective veil of trees. Latina could hear shouts of laughter coming from down by the falls where Dirk had taken Althea to wade in the shallow water.

Turning from her easel, she looked at Tully stretched out in the sun, napping on the smooth rocks. She thought how Dirk had been influenced by Tully: now he too had become sensitive to Althea's needs and demands.

Latina's imagination had been working overtime for the past week, dreaming of how she would respond to Tully's invitation for another picnic. But it was Jayleen who'd suggested it.

"The little one's been raring to go on another picnic, Latina," Jayleen said. "Could you and Dirk go this Saturday? I know it'd be fine with Tully."

When Tully had arrived to pick them up, she was still wrestling with questions of where his feelings for her actually stood. Now whenever he smiled at her, her heart did crazy, wild things, and her mouth went cottony dry. He had never given an indication of affection toward her other than appreciating her help with Althea. Why then the unexplainable ache within her? The intense longing to see him and to hear his husky voice speak her name? It was all so crazy.

She squinted against the sunlight filtering through the dense trees, which had transformed the water to a rare shade of emerald. Swirling her brush in the greens of her palette, she struggled to duplicate the scene on her canvas.

Presently, Tully roused himself and grinned sheepishly as though embarrassed at having fallen asleep.

"Welcome back," she said teasingly.

"Too much good food and warm sun. An icy dip will fix that." He retreated behind the boulders to strip to his swim trunks before mounting the high rocks and diving into the water. Surfacing, he called for her to join him.

"Just a sec," she replied, wanting to finish a bit more before quitting. Her dive into the frigid spring water was not as graceful as his, and she was gasping from cold as her head bobbed up. "Feels like the North Sea!" she said between chattering teeth.

"You'll get used to it."

"Your dive was beautiful," she told him.

"Dad taught me. We used to spend hours here together."

"He must have been a great swimmer, too."

"The best."

"Will you show me what I'm doing wrong?"

"I'd be obliged."

Together, they climbed back up on the rocks and he pointed out flaws in her form and push-off. Later, they swam closer to the mill, where she could see the huge waterwheel reflected in the pond.

Suddenly, without warning, Latina was dragged under water without a split-second to swallow a precious gulp of air. She felt herself being sucked down, down, down. Stabbing pains cut into her chest. There was an eternity of spinning and sinking, of blackness and pain. She felt that her lungs would burst.

A strong arm wound itself around her neck and she felt herself being carried up through the swirling water to the blessed warm sunshine. She gasped as the first breath of air filled her lungs. Coughing and spluttering, she clung to Tully as he lifted her up to the bank. Placing her carefully on the sunbaked rock, he hefted himself up beside her.

"A whirlpool," he explained, amid heavy gasps of air. "Sorry I had to grab you like that. It happened too fast to warn you."

Gradually, she began to breathe more evenly. He placed his hand over hers and kneeled over her. "I almost..." his voice caught, "I almost lost you."

Through half-closed eyes, she saw his face come closer to hers. She felt his lips gently brush her forehead. "Latina-Flower, you gave me a terrible fright."

"That makes twice you've had to rescue me," she just had time to whisper before Dirk burst in on them shouting, "Hey you guys! What happened?"

"Let's go out to the garden and pick your mama a mess of tomatoes," Donna Dee said to Latina one evening when she arrived at the Garwood home. "I need to talk to you private-like! Alone! Now!"

"Sure," Latina agreed. "Mom would love some more tomatoes."

When they reached the garden, Latina noticed Donna Dee hadn't brought a sack for the tomatoes. "What's ailin' you, child?" she said in a friendly imitation of Etta Ann.

Donna Dee laughed a little and took a deep breath. "Latina, do you believe in love at first sight?"

"At first sight?" Latina paused, remembering how she had despised Tully when she had first looked upon his laughing eyes at Boles's Grocery. "I don't know. I suppose it could happen."

"It has, Latina! It has! To me!"

"*You?*"

"Yes, me. Of all people." She took a little whirl down the tomato row. "Brad Jenner and I are in love.

Oh, Latina. He's so wonderful! So wonderful! I know he's the right one for me! And look." From her jean's pocket, she drew out the most delicate diamond ring Latina had ever seen. She slipped it on her finger and held it up to admire it in the last rays of sunlight.

"You and Brad? What about you and Tully?" The cry of her heart tumbled out of her mouth before she could prevent it.

"Tully? You thought Tully was sweet on me all this time? Why honey, I'm a full two years older than that boy! He's like my little brother. I've known Tully all my life."

She placed her hand on Latina's arm. "I've noticed the way you look at him lately, though. I guess this really *is* good news for you, isn't it?"

Latina blushed. "Hey, we're getting off the subject. It's you that's all giddy and cow-eyed."

Latina remembered the Fourth of July when she'd watched the two of them walking together. Donna Dee had probably been talking to Tully about Brad Jenner!

"Listen, Latina," Donna Dee was saying, "I'm going to need your support. The law firm has decided to move Brad and his cousin upstate to open another office, and Brad will be leaving. He's asked me to marry him before he leaves. I don't know what Mama and Daddy will say. They might think I can't be sure in such a short time. But I'm sure! More sure than I've ever been about anything. Will you stay with me while

I tell them? You've been such a dear to me this summer. I've never had a friend so close."

Latina gave Dona Dee a hug. "You're the greatest, Donna Dee. It's no wonder that the young lawyer lost his heart over you. I bet he still doesn't know what hit him."

It was her friend's turn to blush. "Well, are you with me or not?"

"Through thick and thin," Latina said. Hooking her arm into Donna Dee's, they walked back to the house.

"Mother, you'll never guess what," Latina said, pulling up a chair beside her mother and collapsing into it. "Donna Dee's fallen in love with the young lawyer in her office and she's getting married right away. We're all invited to the wedding. It's to be held at the Zell's Bush Community Church."

"Just a minute," her mother protested, placing the Afghan that she was crocheting in the tapestry bag at her feet. "Slow down and begin at the beginning. You're going too fast."

To begin at the beginning, Latina thought, would mean telling how she had thought that Donna Dee and Tully were more than friends, and how excited she was to learn that wasn't true at all. But this wasn't the right time to tell it. As briefly as possible, she told Donna Dee's news.

She wondered what her mother would think of such a short courtship and was relieved to hear her say,

"Why, that's wonderful news! I'm pleased the girl is marrying someone who can support her. So many of the young people in these parts seem to be trapped here. But I could tell Donna Dee was different."

"Like Tully?"

"Like Tully." Her mother gazed for a moment out past the backyard into the trees behind the Nettleton house. "That Tully's a whiz and he's covering material quickly. He'll be ready for college by second semester at least."

"Mom, why haven't you and Dad encouraged Tully to attend a college nearer home?"

"Your father and I feel since we'll both be there at Eagleton, we'll be able to give him more assistance than if he were among strangers. Actually, the decision is up to him. He's looked at the brochures and catalogs we've shown him, and he loves the idea."

But what would college life do to his personality, Latina wondered. How would he endure dorm life after roaming the untamed hills, nursing wild animals and diving from the rocks at the millpond? And who would save the animals from the clutches of the steel traps?

"You're not too sure about all this are you, dear?"

"It's Jayleen," she explained. That was partly true. Thinking a minute, she added, "Mom, could we buy them a gift to help out?"

"Gift? What kind of gift?"

"I've been thinking about how hard it is to travel with Althea and I thought a car seat might help."

Her mother smiled. "That's a great idea, Latina. She's bigger than a toddler though. We'd have to get a sturdy one."

"Would it be expensive?" Latina knew their finances had been pretty short that summer.

"It would, but I think your father will feel it's worth it. And I agree wholeheartedly."

"Can we shop for it tomorrow? I'd like you to help me pick it out."

"It's a date!"

On the way to Palatka the next day, Latina found herself opening up and sharing with her mother more than she had for a long time, especially when the subject turned to her painting.

"There's still so much I don't know." Latina had kicked off her sandals and sat curled up in the rider's side. It was good to have her mom negotiating the hills for a change. She had never liked the hairpin curves. "I was wondering if I could fit an art class into my fall schedule."

"Good idea. We can call in a week or so to see what's available."

Latina stared at the trees whipping by. "I'm going to miss everyone a lot," she admitted.

"We all are." Pauline turned a tight curve while meeting a semi-trailer. Then she said, "The summer turned out better than you had thought. Right?"

Latina nodded. "I've learned so much about so many things. Just meeting Althea has been an experience in itself."

"You're quite taken with her, aren't you?"

"She's so easy to love. I keep thinking there must be scores of children like her everywhere who need someone to understand them." Without planning to, Latina spoke the thoughts that had been growing in her mind. "Mom, I'd like to be like Beverly Wilkes—someone who is there to help and to understand. I want to learn to teach handicapped children. Beverly not only teaches Althea, but she's a help to Jayleen as well."

For the first time in her life, Latina felt a sense of purpose. It was an exhilarating discovery.

Rosie, the coon hound, silently padded up to Latina and licked her hand as she stepped up to the Clouse's front door. Tully answered her knock. "Latina-Flower! Come on in here. Althea's napping, but I can get her," he said.

"No," she protested. "Don't wake her."

"Come on in," Jayleen called to her from the far side of the kitchen. "Pleased to see you."

"I, uh, I've brought something for you. It's in the car." Had she ignorantly assumed too much? The Clouses were a proud family, not given to receiving charity. Would they think she was feeling sorry for them? Perhaps she should have asked them first. Tully might even think she'd bought the gift to make an impression on him.

"You have something for us, you say?" Jayleen came toward her, wiping her hands on a faded dish towel. "Whatever could it be?" she asked, openly curious.

"You'll see." Looking up at Tully, she said, "It's in the trunk. I'll need your help."

"I'm with you." He followed her into the warm night.

She hoped he didn't detect the trembling in her fingers as she turned the key in the trunk lock. As the dim light of the trunk illuminated the large box with obvious pictures and writing on the outside, Tully was suddenly silent.

"It's for Althea," her words were barely above a whisper. "From our family to yours. So Jayleen can take her places alone."

She forced herself to turn and look up at him. "Um, you'll have to carry it," she said. "It's pretty awkward."

She was touched to see tears glistening on his cheeks.

"Latina-Flower, you tell your fine family we're mighty grateful." He stood there a moment, his eyes fixed on the box. She was amazed at his unashamedness at the free-flowing tears. Unbidden, her hand reached up to his cheek to brush one away. The ache within her to touch him was overwhelming.

He reached out and took her hand and pressed it against his face.

"Let's go show Mama!" he said suddenly, lifting up the box and closing the trunk with a slam.

Jayleen shed tears of joy as she opened the box. "Latina, we're so grateful to you. Whooo! It's a pretty one, isn't it?" she said, pulling it from the box. "There's no way we could ever say thanks good enough."

"You already have, Jayleen. By just being yourselves. I've learned so much from having known you."

"Oh pawsh! We're just common folk. But this—this is so grand." She ran her fingers over the padded seat. "Won't it be great to have Althea ride in this, Tully? Why, we could even set her in it here in the house. Won't she be as fine as any little girl sitting in this?" With that, she began to set it up there on the couch.

"It's perfect, Mama," Tully agreed. "Perfect."

As his mother busied herself with the mechanics of the car seat, Tully turned to Latina. "I've got to drive up to Campton Corners this evening to get some parts for Garwood's saw from another mill. In fact, I should have left before now. Want to ride along?"

"Why, I'd love to, Tully," she managed to say above her beating heart.

Their conversation along the way was easy and light. Tully asked several questions about Eagleton College that she was unable to answer, even though she'd lived near the campus all her life. It struck her how she'd taken for granted the fact that college was to be her destination. For Tully, it was still an intangible dream.

"How will Jayleen manage once you've gone?" She finally asked the inevitable question that had been persistently nagging at her.

"We've talked about it a lot, Latina. I guess leaving her alone with Althea will be the hardest thing I've ever done. But your parents are opening a door for me that I thought was closed forever. If I don't go through it now, I may miss the chance completely."

"You'll still be here in the summer?"

"I think so. But winters are hardest. Keeping the wood cut and all."

"Can't some of the neighbors help?"

"Some will, but it's not enough. I'll have to see to it that the supply is in before I leave. A full winter's supply."

"What does Jayleen say about your leaving?"

"She's tickled pink. She's been pushing me to go from the first moment I mentioned it. 'We'll get along,' she says. 'The Lord'll watch over us every day. You wait and see.'"

Latina could just hear her saying it. "She's little but mighty, isn't she?"

"I reckon she is, Latina. I reckon she is."

Campton Corners was a town much like Zell's Bush. It took only a few minutes for Tully to locate the mill and get the part.

On the way home, Tully pulled up to a gas station where the lights out front wore hazy yellow halos. Through dust-dimmed windows, Latina could see him feeding coins into a decrepit pop machine. As she lay her head back on the pickup seat, she thought that even in the smartest places Periwinkle Cove had to offer, she'd never been this happy.

He opened the creaking pickup door and handed her the chilled, damp can and slid behind the wheel. Once out on the road, he surprised her by asking, "What do you hear from that guy back East? Old what's-his-name?"

She hadn't thought of Kent for weeks. "You mean Kent?"

"Oh, yeah. Kent, it was. You hear from him?"

"Um..." She took a sip of soda.

"Well?"

"Well, what?"

"About hearing from that Kent fellow."

"I haven't heard," she admitted.

"Not at all?"

"Not at all."

"Not even a note or a call?"

"Not a line. Not a word."

Tully sipped his soda pop and drove around through the endless hills and valleys. "You think I upset him?"

Boy, did you, she wanted to say. And so did I. She waited a minute before answering. Awkwardly, she caught at the door handle so she wouldn't slide across the seat as they took a hairpin curve. "Something must have upset him," she offered.

"He upset easily?"

"I hadn't thought so—until he came to Zell's Bush."

"Zell's Bush has a refining fire you go through. Tests the mettle to see what you're made of. Some just can't handle it." His eyes were laughing now. She could see them by the reflection of the dash lights.

"Are you the refining fire?"

"Me? Heavens no!" he retorted. "It's the hills."

"The hills, huh?"

"They make you or break you."

Don't they though! She remembered how ominous and threatening they had been to her in the beginning. "And what about me?" she wanted to know. "Has my mettle been refined?"

"Latina," he answered in his soft husky voice, "you've passed with flying colors!"

At that moment, another corner caught her unaware, causing her to slide and fall over against him. Tossing his empty pop can to the floor, he freed his hand to place an arm about her and pull her closer. "Are we gonna have to get you a car seat like Althea's to hold you in?" he asked. "Or do you mind if I do the job?"

Mind? She had never been so happy.

# Chapter Eleven

Latina attempted to read Parke Garwood's reactions to her paintings by watching his eyes. They were sitting in the Garwoods' living room and the paintings, now mounted in oak frames, were propped up on the coffee table. That is, Etta Ann and Latina were sitting, Mr. Garwood was pacing.

Presently, he stopped and looked at the paintings once again, then spoke. "We're obliged to you, Latina. When I look at the mill in a picture like this, it sorta gives me a broader outlook on things. Like getting out of my skin and looking at myself to get things figured out. Know what I mean?"

She did indeed. Latina had been doing a great deal of soul searching herself the past few weeks. She nodded.

"We appreciate the work you've done for us," he repeated, "but more than that, I'm proud of what you've done for Jayleen Clouse." He was standing at the other end of the small room now, staring out the window. "I saw that thingamajig you bought for the little one to sit in when she rides." He ran short fingers through his hair. "I'm downright ashamed none of us here in Zell's Bush ever thought of such a thing."

It was difficult to know how to reply. She hadn't given the gift in order to make others in the community feel guilty.

Etta Ann went to the kitchen to fix iced cider, then returned to sit down again. Mr. Garwood continued to pace the close quarters of the living room, his boots going soft and then loud as he stepped on and off the braided rug that was spread out on the hardwood floor.

"I understand Tully may be clearing out of here come winter. Donna Dee told us about his studies. I've been trying to help as much as I can by giving the boy extra jobs to do."

Silence fell again and Latina was uncomfortable. It was a sultry afternoon. Few people in Zell's Bush had air conditioning and the Garwood's living room was stifling. Latina wondered how she could politely slip away, but Mr. Garwood seemed intent on having this serious visit. She had thought she would simply drop the paintings off and leave quickly. She never dreamed he would abandon the saws in the middle of the afternoon and come to visit with her.

"And another thing," Mr. Garwood went on as though he'd never stopped. "Etta and me, we've been discussing something. Before you came to Zell's Bush, we never gave a thought to the little Clouse girl. We sorta felt it best they keep her tucked away and let her grow up best she could. But you've made us think there could be more to her life than being hidden away."

Now it was Mr. Garwood's turn to be uncomfortable. Perspiration beaded on his forehead as he groped for words.

"What he's trying to say, Latina," Etta Ann came to his rescue, "is that we want to do more than just help Tully. Now that Donna Dee is leaving us—the last of our three girls—we thought it'd be nice to have someone else around. We'd like to build Jayleen and Althea a place right here." Etta Ann waved a plump arm toward the side of the house. "Out there on the ridge up from the garden would be a cozy spot. That way we could look after them when Tully's gone."

Mr. Garwood pulled out a red handkerchief to wipe his brow. "We can't hardly expect Tully to return from college and settle down in that cabin the rest of his life just because of a handicapped sister."

"Do they know?" Latina asked.

"Not yet," Mr. Garwood answered. "As a matter of fact, we just decided last evening, after seeing the little one sitting so happy in that fancy riding seat in Tully's truck." He rubbed the stubble on his chin thoughtfully. "That really did get to me."

Latina pressed her hands against the cold, wet glass of cider. If she were home she would have rubbed it on her forehead. "Why are you telling me first?"

Etta Ann's round face gave a wide smile. "Because you were the cause of it all. You opened our eyes."

"Aaron Clouse built their house." Latina's mind was racing. "Do you think Jayleen will want to leave it?"

Mr. Garwood perched himself in the worn, over-stuffed chair, his elbows propped on his knees. "We're not sure. All we can do is ask and see."

"May I..." Latina began, then wondered why she was even asking. This was none of her affair. "May I be the one to tell them of your offer?" She blurted it out quickly, before she could change her mind.

Parke's eyes shifted first to Etta Ann, then back to her. "I'd be obliged if you would. I find it a hard thing to talk about." Mr. Harwood heaved a relieved sigh! "I'll write you that check for the paintings. You've certainly earned it—in more ways than one."

The petunias in the washtub on the Clouse's front porch were now a jungle of vivid pinks, orchids and royal purples. Their gentle fragrances wafted toward Latina as she knocked at the front door. She recalled the first night she came here, soaking wet in Tully's arms. The petunias had been tiny green spikes.

Her heart jumped to see the blue pickup parked in the yard, but it was Althea who pushed the screen open. "Huw-wo Ah-teen-a. Wuv Ah-teen-a."

"I saw it was you," Jayleen said from her rocking chair, "so I let her answer."

Latina stepped inside and knelt to hold Althea close. She looked out, wondering where Tully was.

"He's out checking the traps," Jayleen said with a knowing smile that made Latina blush. "Should be back any minute. Come in and set a spell. I'm needing to ask a favor of you."

"Anything," Latina said, carrying Althea with her to the couch.

"Miss Wilkes has invited me to come to an all-day affair for parents of handicapped children next Friday. I was wondering if Althea could spend the day with you?"

All day. Jayleen trusted her to take Althea all day. "I'd love to have her, Jayleen. You know I would."

"Thanks, Latina." Her eyes were bright and clear, like Tully's. "This is going to be a grand time for me. Meeting other folks who have the same problems to face as I do. I'm going to learn so much."

"You'll be the most well-adjusted one there," Latina said with a laugh. "They'll be asking you for advice."

Jayleen glowed under the compliment, but said in her usual way, "Oh pawsh!"

"How will you get there?"

"Miss Wilkes is driving all the way up here to get me. Don't that beat all? I told her she didn't have to do that, but she wouldn't take no for an answer. She thinks I need to be at some meetings like this, and she also thinks..." Jayleen stopped and studied the sock she was mending. "She thinks since Tully's leaving, it might be good for me to find a place in Palatka to live, where I'd be closer to people who could help me. She's even offered to help me find a little place."

"What did you tell her?"

Jayleen looked at her intently. "I'm a little mixed up, Latina. I want to do what's best for Althea, and I'm not sure being stuck away up here is the answer."

The slam of the back door announced Tully's return and sent Latina's heart pounding.

Althea jumped down out of Latina's lap and made a dash for her brother's legs. He swooped down and caught her and lifted her toward the ceiling amid an explosion of giggles.

Then he sent a smile to Latina that she knew was meant for her alone. Some unspoken expression passed between them that was too deep for words. "Howdy, Latina."

"Hi. I've been waiting for you to come in before I shared the good news."

"Whoo-wee! You hear that talk, Althea? Good news! I'm all for that." He folded himself into a nearby chair with Althea still nestled in his arms.

Latina hoped this news would be what they needed to hear. If Beverly had approached Jayleen about moving, it meant she'd already been considering making major changes in her life.

As briefly as possible, Latina told them of the Garwoods' offer to build a small house for Jayleen and Althea on the ridge above the Etta Ann's garden. She explained that Mr. Garwood wanted to do something to help Althea develop as much as was possible. And that he and Etta Ann wanted to be able to look after them now that Donna Dee and Tully would both be leaving.

The room grew quiet. Jayleen's rocker ceased its creaking. "That would truly be the answer to my prayers," she said with wonder in her voice.

Tully was shaking his head in disbelief. "Garwood was always such a hard old bruiser. I never considered that he gave us a passing thought. A house by the sawmill. Sure would be handy, Mama. I reckon I could even help on the building of it this fall before I leave in January."

"I wasn't sure you'd want to leave this house," Latina put in. "I know it's special to you."

"It is special, Latina," Jayleen agreed. "*Right* special. But so is Althea, and I want to do what's best for her and for her future."

Tully was still in a daze. "Close to other houses," he said slowly. "Why you and Etta Ann'll be chatting all the time! And whevever you feel like getting a cold soda pop, you can walk up to Boles's and be there in a whipstitch."

Althea sensed something was in the air; she giggled and bounced on Tully's knees.

Latina felt it was time to leave and let mother and son work out all these details privately. As she excused herself and rose to go, Tully said, "Latina, I've been thinking. It's high time for us to have another picnic at the millpond—just you and me."

Latina felt warmth rise to her cheeks. No boy she'd ever known would have asked a girl for a date in front of his mother. "It *is* high time, isn't it?" she said. "Exactly which high time did you have in mind?"

"My calendar tells me we won't have too many more Saturdays. How about this next one?"

Her throat went dry. Summer was nearly over. "This Saturday for sure," she said.

"I'll be down to get you at eleven."

"And," Jayleen added, "I'll have Althea there by eight on Friday morning."

"Saturday it is, Latina-Flower," Tully said. His clear blue eyes were filled with happiness.

When Latina told her parents of Mr. Garwood's offer to Tully's family, her father was surprised.

"Who would have thought that hard-nosed businessman would do such a thing?" he said. "What made him think of it?"

"He said when he saw Althea so happy in that thingamajig, he realized she needed more than to be stuck away up in the hills alone."

Latina's mother was as excited about the offer as Jayleen had been. "It'll make life so much easier for Tully away at school," she said, "knowing his family is being cared for."

"Do you think," Latina asked, struggling with her perplexing thoughts, "that life on campus will spoil Tully? He has such, such..." Latina groped for the right words, "golden qualities."

Her father gave his pipe a few soft puffs. "Tully's golden qualities, as you call them, run deep in Tully, Latina. I can't believe he will tarnish that easily. In fact, I think that others about him will bask in the reflected light of it. Right, Paulie?"

"Yes," her mother agreed with a smile, "Tully will be great for Eagleton College."

They could bask in the reflected light of Tully's golden qualities, Latina thought, just as I do.

The phone rang. It was Donna Dee for Latina.

"So you're not shopping late in Palatka tonight?" Latina asked.

"Not tonight. I came straight home after work, but on Friday, I have scads of things to do. Brad talked his daddy into letting me have the entire day off. Latina, could you drive me to Palatka on Friday? I just found out that Daddy needs our car."

After checking with her parents, Latina assured Donna Dee she'd be available. "Oh, wait a minute!" She stopped, suddenly remembering. "I have to keep Althea on Friday."

"Well, bring her along. She's no trouble."

Latina hesitated. The understanding was that Althea would be staying here at the house during the day. It didn't seem right to make other plans without letting Jayleen know, but since they didn't have a phone...

"I really need you," Donna Dee was saying on the other end. "Jayleen knows you'll take care of Althea no matter where you are."

"I suppose you're right. She loves to travel, that's for sure."

What a busy week this was turning out to be, Latina mused as she replaced the receiver in its cradle. And crowning it all was her picnic alone with Tully on Saturday. She could hardly wait!

The car seat made transporting Althea infinitely easier, although noisier, as she made ample use of the squeaky horn hidden in the padded safety bar. At times, she remembered the horn on the steering wheel, and crying, "Honk! Honk!" she strained to reach it.

Repeatedly, throughout the course of the day, Latina spoke to her gently, "Althea's horn," and patted the safety bar. Then, "Latina's horn," pointing to the steering wheel. "No, no. No touch Latina's horn."

Beaming, Althea would give her head a shake, "No, no!" and honk her squeaky horn again.

Donna Dee laughed, then plugged her fingers in her ears. "I hope my eardrums survive all these lessons," she said. Then she added, "You do wonders with her, Latina. I've known her all her life and I never thought to try to teach her anything. I don't know how you do it."

"I'm not exactly sure either," Latina admitted. "It just seems to come to me."

Late that afternoon, Donna Dee had only one more stop to make—that of the home of her future in-laws. She wanted to leave some parcels there as the Garwood home was being overcrowded with all her new acquisitions.

Latina and Althea waited in the car in front of the fine two-story home situated on the outskirts of Palatka. Presently, the bride-to-be came out to the car with a worried expression. "Latina, Mrs. Jenner's not feeling well, and Brad and his father are gone on a business trip for the night."

"I'm sorry to hear that. Is there anything we can do?"

"Well, if you don't mind awfully, I've offered to stay the night with her. Brad can drive me home tomorrow afternoon."

Latina didn't relish the thought of driving back to Zell's Bush alone with Althea, but confessing it would only make her friend feel bad. "Of course you stay with her, Donna Dee. She needs you."

"Thanks, Latina. You're an understanding dear. Please come in for a while. Mrs. Jenner wanted me to invite you in for a snack before you go."

Mrs. Jenner was gracious to them in spite of feeling weak. She was kindly tolerant of Althea and overlooked falling cake crumbs on the gold-flowered kitchen carpet.

Much of the conversation centered around the work of the law firm and the upcoming wedding, which left Latina somewhat in the dark. She was anxious to get home before nightfall, so she excused herself as soon as possible.

Donna Dee walked her to the car and asked, "Latina, would you mind stopping at the house and telling Mama and Daddy where I am? No sense in making long-distance phone calls from here."

"No problem. It's on our way. Right, Althea?"

The little girl rocked back and forth in her car seat, anxious to be on the move again. She'd quickly become an avid traveler.

"Thanks again, Latina. How can I ever repay you for all you're doing for me?"

Latina settled herself behind the wheel. "Friends don't worry about paying back, do they?"

Donna Dee gave her arm a squeeze. "No, Latina. No, they don't."

When Latina drove out past the Palatka city limits, the sky held the last pink tints of daylight. She and Althea chattered to each other until at last, Althea lay her head on the padded bar and fell soundly asleep.

It was dark by the time they reached Zell's Bush. Only the Coca-Cola sign in Boles's window and the bare bulbs glowing in front of the gas station gave hints of civilization. Latina wondered if Jayleen had returned home yet and hoped she wouldn't be worried about Althea. She certainly hadn't planned to be this late in getting back.

She noticed as she stopped the car by the sawmill that there were no lights on up at the house. Evidently, the Garwoods had gone somewhere together and weren't back yet. She'd have to leave a note for them on the front door.

Switching on the car's interior light she rummaged in her purse for a scrap of paper and pen. Althea was still asleep. After she'd scribbled out the note, Latina looked up at the silent house perched on the ridge.

She'd never seen it so dark and deserted. Shadows under the sheds gave them an eerie appearance.

Perhaps she could call the Garwoods later from her house. She switched the light off once again and reached to turn the key in the ignition. But what would Etta Ann think when she got home and Donna Dee wasn't there? She'd be needlessly frightened.

"This is foolishness," she chided herself sternly. "I'll run up there, fasten a note to the door and be on my way in no time. There's absolutely nothing to be afraid of."

Stepping from the air-conditioned car, she was surprised to find the air sultry and still. A summer storm was brewing. The heavy smell of freshly cut wood hung thick in the air. She pushed the car door closed until it barely clicked so the slam wouldn't disturb Althea.

Her steps echoed as she walked up the winding path. In the distance, a whippoorwill cried. Ragged clouds swept by the moon. The front door screen was locked, but she was able to slip the note into the wooden screen door so that a corner was visible. She could only hope they would see it.

She made her way back down toward the car when a sudden movement under the big shed caught her eye.

"Hey there! Latina-Flower!"

She'd have known that high-pitched, whining voice anywhere. It was Collier!

In an uncontrolled panic, she broke into a wild, frantic race for the car. As she did, his heavy footsteps sounded also, running from the sheds toward her. If only she could make it to the car and lock the door before he reached her.

The heat pressed in against her so that her lungs could scarcely function. A searing pain burned into her side. Her feet were barely touching the path. Collier's dark form was coming at her fast.

Terrified now, she grabbed at the partially opened door and flung herself into the seat. But he yanked at the door and pulled it from her grip before she could slam it in his face.

# Chapter Twelve

Now where're you going in such an all-fired hurry?"
Collier asked.

Latina rubbed her sore fingers, which had been en-
twined in the door handle as he forced it open. "Let
go, Collier. I've got to get Althea home. She's tired
and Jayleen's expecting us."

The fracas had awakened Althea and at the sight of
Collier, she began to whimper.

"Hey! You got the dimwit. Ain't this handy." He
gave a lopsided grin. Roughly, he grabbed Latina's
arm and tried to pull her from behind the wheel.
"Come out of there. I gotta talk to you."

"Leave us alone!" she cried out, fighting against
him. As she braced herself, she thought of the keys

and knew instinctively she must keep them from him. Twisting around, she managed to get her foot positioned to kick him hard. As she did, she slipped the keys out of the ignition and into her slacks pocket.

He yelped at the kick and his anger only increased his strength. She felt herself being dragged from the car. She stumbled, then caught her balance and stood frightened before him. His hand clenched her wrist. His dark eyes burned with anger.

"You ain't going nowhere, Latina-Flower. I need your help to get away. Tonight, I evened things up and now I got to get away from this place. I'm getting out of here for good."

"Evened things up? How?" If she could keep him talking, perhaps the Garwoods would drive in. Let them hurry, she prayed silently. Above all else, she had to see that Althea was safe.

"Look here," he said, pulling a wad of bills from his pocket. "This makes up for all the times Tully got raises in pay and I didn't get none. And when he got extra jobs and I never got anything. It ain't fair that Tully's everybody's little pet, and everybody hates old Collier."

So, he'd robbed the mill office, and now he was planning to run!

"That's not true, Collier." She forced a steadiness into her voice. "People like you, too."

With a quick, strong jerk, he flipped her arm painfully behind her back and pulled her up against his chest. "Is that right, Latina-Flower? You're lying and you know it. You don't like me. You hate me. You knew I killed the stupid old coon and you hated me for it, didn't you?''

She wanted to scream yes in his face. She'd hated him from the first moment she'd laid eyes on him. Struggling, she tried to kick at his shins, but he pulled her arm tighter until she thought it would surely break. A groan escaped her lips, frightening Althea even more.

''Whatever you want me to do, Collier, I'll do it. But please let Althea go. You're frightening her.''

''She don't know enough whether to be scared or not. And I got news for you, Miss Snooty City Girl, you're going to do what I say no matter what! You're going to drive me away from this place where all these people hate me. They hated my daddy and brothers, and now they hate me. I should have left long ago.''

''I'll drive you anywhere, Collier. Just let me take Althea up to the house first....''

''Be quiet now! I got to get things figured out here.'' As he spoke, Latina sensed the pressure on her arm easing ever so slightly. With a burst of new strength, she wrenched from his grasp. She fished for the keys in her pocket and threw them as hard as she could into the brush at the edge of the parking lot.

''Why, you hair-brained dummy. That was the keys! That was my way out of here!''

Latina wanted to run, but there was no way she could leave Althea with this crazy guy. Glaring at her, Collier slowly reached down and slipped a knife out of

his work boots. "This here's my skinning knife, Latina. I keep it sharper than my whittling knife. Now
you get over there and find them keys."

She stared terror-stricken at the glinting knife, remembering Coony's lifeless body on the grass. "It will
take a while," she said. "Mr. Garwood could drive in
here any minute and catch you. Then what would you
do?"

He snorted a curse under his breath. "I don't need
the likes of you anyhow. All I need is one hostage to
get me out of here. The dimwit'll do just fine. I know
these hills like the palm of my hand and I'll walk out
of here faster than spit on a hot skillet. You'll see."

Once again, he grabbed her arm. "You come with
me!" He marched her ahead of him along the path,
through the dark tunnels of sheds and into the moonlight on the other side. She was half-pushed, half-
pulled to the brick toolshed.

"I'm leaving you here so you can tell them all that
I got a hostage. You tell them, Latina. You tell them
if anyone comes after me or tries to stop me, I'll hurt
the dimwit real bad. You hear?" Keeping a tight hold
on her forearms, he fumbled with the bolted door.

"No Collier! Not in there! I promise I won't leave!
I'll stay right here. I'll tell them for you. I won't even
follow you. Please don't put me in there!"

"Can't trust anyone now, Latina-Flower." He
closed the door with a bang.

She caught the sound of Althea's crying and managed to get hold of herself to listen for the direction of

their departure. Toward the woods on the far side of the road, it seemed. But in the oven-like toolshed, filled with acrid odors of oil and grease, how could she trust her own senses? He might have taken her up into the hills behind the house.

On her feet now, she shoved her body against the door several times, but she only succeeded in knocking the wind out of herself. Groping around for something to use to pound on the door, her hands met with a curtain of sticky cobwebs. When she located a long wooden handle that turned out to be a shovel, she used it to hit at the door, but this attempt was also useless. Thoroughly fatigued now, she sat down on the cool floor to wait. She mustn't panic. It couldn't be much longer before the Garwoods returned, and Althea would be rescued. She hoped it wouldn't be too late.

Then she heard a faint cry in the distance. She strained intently to hear it more clearly. It was a pitiful wail like that of a wounded animal.

She jumped to her feet again. She had to get out! Now her eyes were accustomed to the dark, aided by open vents near the ceiling that let in the dim moonlight, and she spied a sledgehammer.

Straining at its weight, she groaned in an attempt to swing at the door near the point where the latch was located. Nothing. Again came the wailing, pitiful cry.

If Collier had hurt Althea, she'd see to it he was put away forever!

It was the third swing of the heavy tool that loosened the latch and set her free. Instantly, she was out and running, stumbling up the rutted drive, across the road and into the woods following the sounds of the cries. She knew now that it wasn't Althea who was hurt. The words were too clear. "Please help! Somebody help me!"

It was Collier.

"I'm coming," she called back. "Where are you? Althea! Althea, where are you?"

Pushing through the underbrush in the darkness, Latina felt the briars clawing at her clothing and her bare arms and face. At last, she heard Althea's answer and saw her coming over a ridge in her rolling gait. "At-teen-a! Ah-teen-a!"

Breaking into a run, Latina met the girl and lifted her into her arms comforting her whimpers and pushing on through the trees. Collier's soft moans were just over the hill.

There on the floor of a leaf-carpeted ravine he lay writhing in the damp leaves, his ankle crushed in one of his own traps.

"Oh, thank God, Latina! You came to me. Please, please help me! It hurts awful. I can't stand the pain. Please help me!"

His own trap—and a big one! Not like the small one Dirk nearly fell into. She looked at the bloody ankle, then turned sharply away.

"We'll go back to the mill and phone for help, Collier. I'll run as fast as I can."

"No! Oh, no. Please don't leave me, Latina. I'm scared. Get it off me. Please."

Remembering how Tully's strong hands struggled to open the one they found at the millpond, she knew there was no hope of freeing him herself. "I can't Collier. There's no way I could open it." Her voice was soft and steady. She studied the chain securely fastened around a nearby oak tree.

"I'm so scared. Please don't leave me."

Taking Althea by the shoulders and looking directly into her eyes, she instructed. "Althea, go to the car at the mill. To the car, Althea." She pointed in the direction of the sawmill. "Latina's horn, Althea. Latina's horn. Honk! Honk!"

Althea's eyes brightened. With her thin hand, she mimed the honking, then laughed.

"That's right, Althea. That's a good girl! Honk Latina's horn and don't stop. Don't stop! Hold it and hold it! Now go!"

Althea headed off through the woods toward the road.

Collier's groan subsided. Latina moved toward him. She seated herself in the damp hollow of ground and laid his head on her lap.

"I'm sorry," he gasped. "I wouldn't listen about the traps. I knew all along it wasn't right. Tully tried and tried to tell me."

"Sh," she hushed him. "Don't try to talk." She stroked the dark hair as though it had been Dirk lying there.

Suddenly the car horn began to blare. "She's doing it, ain't she?" Collier whispered. "How'd she know to do that?"

"That cousin of yours is one smart little girl, Collier."

"I never claimed her as kin before. Didn't want no dimwit for any kin of mine. I didn't know she could understand stuff."

"She sure can. And she can love a lot too!"

Tears were coursing their way down Collier's face onto her soiled slacks. She wiped his face with the shirt tail of her blouse.

Thunder rumbled behind them as Latina's eyes searched the darkness. Once again Collier groaned. "The pain, Latina. It's awful."

"Squeeze my hand," she said. Placing her hand in his, she let him squeeze.

"It helps," he said. "It really helps."

His young face was ivory against his black hair. How could she have been afraid of him? He was a hurt young man crying out for love and acceptance. Tully had seen it all along.

"How'd you get out of the shed?"

"Sledgehammer."

"Geez," he breathed. "You're really something." There was a long pause and then, "You could have left me." His words were barely audible.

It was only a few minutes later that Latina heard approaching footsteps.

Tully reached her first, although she could tell by the commotion there were others following.

"Latina! Are you all right?" Soon he was by her side, his arms about her, looking into her face, placing kisses on her forehead and cheeks.

"I'm okay, Tully. But your cousin here needs a helping hand."

Latina had never seen Orville Boles move so fast, and to see him come galloping through the woods was comical in spite of the circumstances. Parke Garwood was right beside him.

The three of them working together freed Collier from the wicked teeth of the trap. Orville and Parke gently carried the moaning boy back through the trees. Tully helped Latina up from the wet ground. She was gripped by a violent trembling that she'd resisted for many hours. The first fat raindrops began to slap against the leaves and onto their hair and faces. Tully pulled off his shirt and placed it around her shoulders and held her close as they made their way out of the underbrush.

"Althea's all right?" she asked anxiously.

"She's with Etta Ann and she's fine. Proud of her honking job. I had just gone up to Boles's to watch for you when we heard it. Parke was pulling in the drive when Orville and I got here. Perfect timing."

Latina sighed with relief.

In the Garwood's kitchen, Etta Ann wrapped Latina in a lavender knitted Afghan. "You're in no condition to drive, young lady," Parke announced.

"I couldn't anyway," she said. "I threw the keys into the brush to keep Collier from taking off."

Parke raised a shaggy eyebrow. "Quick thinking."

"Quick thinking for her to tell Althea to honk the horn, too," Etta Ann added.

"Honk! Honk!" Althea proclaimed grandly.

The Garwoods had already phoned the Harmens to tell them what had transpired and learned that Jayleen was there waiting.

Tully rose to his feet. "I planned to take Latina with me and Althea anyway," he said. "I can bring her folks back to get their car later."

The noisy rainstorm had blown away, leaving behind a clean fragrance and a refreshing breeze as the threesome walked down the path to the pickup. One of Tully's arms held Althea, the other encircled Latina's shoulder. "I'm sorry," he said. "I nearly let you get hurt." Slowing for a moment, he bent to kiss her.

"Honk! Honk!" Althea said approvingly.

# The Silhouette
# Cameo Tote Bag
# Now available
# for just $6.99

Handsomely designed in blue and bright pink, its stylish good looks make the Cameo Tote Bag an attractive acces-sory. The Cameo Tote Bag is big and roomy (13″ square), with reinforced handles and a snap-shut top. You can buy the Cameo Tote Bag for $6.99, plus $1.50 for post-age and handling.

Send your name and address with check or money order for $6.99 (plus $1.50 postage and handling), a total of $8.49 to:

**Silhouette Books**
**120 Brighton Road**
**P.O. Box 5084**
**Clifton, NJ 07015-5084**
**ATTN: Tote Bag**

SIL–T–1R

The Silhouette Cameo Tote Bag can be pur-chased pre-paid only. No charges will be accep-ted. Please allow 4 to 6 weeks for delivery.

**N.Y. State Residents Please Add Sales Tax**

Offer not available in Canada.